UNDER
AN
OUTLAW
MOON

UNDER
AN
OUTLAW
MOON

A NOVEL

DIETRICH
KALTEIS

Published by ECW Press
665 Gerrard Street East
Toronto, Ontario, Canada M4M 1Y2
416-694-3348 / info@ecwpress.com

Cover design: Michel Vrana
Author photo: Andrea Kalteis

LIBRARY AND ARCHIVES CANADA CATALOGUING IN
PUBLICATION

Title: Under an outlaw moon : a novel / Dietrich
Kalteis.

Names: Kalteis, Dietrich, 1954- author.

Identifiers: Canadiana (print) 20210238887 |
Canadiana (ebook) 20210238895

ISBN 978-1-77041-547-8 (softcover)
ISBN 978-1-77305-779-8 (ePub)
ISBN 978-1-77305-780-4 (PDF)
ISBN 978-1-77305-781-1 (Kindle)

Classification: LCC PS8621.A474 U53 2021 | DDC
C813/.6—dc23

This book is funded in part by the Government of Canada. *Ce livre est financé en partie par le gouvernement
du Canada.* We acknowledge the support of the Canada Council for the Arts. *Nous remercions le Conseil des
arts du Canada de son soutien.* We acknowledge the support of the Ontario Arts Council (OAC), an agency
of the Government of Ontario, which last year funded 1,965 individual artists and 1,152 organizations in 197
communities across Ontario for a total of $51.9 million. We also acknowledge the support of the Government
of Ontario through Ontario Creates.

 ONTARIO ARTS COUNCIL
CONSEIL DES ARTS DE L'ONTARIO
an Ontario government agency
un organisme du gouvernement de l'Ontario

Canada Council   Conseil des arts
for the Arts   du Canada

PRINTED AND BOUND IN CANADA   PRINTING: FRIESENS   5 4 3 2 1

MIX
Paper from
responsible sources
FSC® C016245

For Wolfgang
Unwavering in his love

Based on the true story of the FBI's most wanted
Bennie and Stella Mae Dickson

...one

JUNE 12, 1937

In the eyes of men I am not just
But in your eyes, O life, I see justification
You have taught me that my path is right if I am true to you.

"Sixteen, huh? Well, I might've guessed older." Flashing her the honest blue eyes.

"Well, maybe you'd'a been wrong then, huh?" Said her name was Stella Mae Redenbaugh, looking at him like she saw something underneath his smile, this guy with the wavy hair, skating around the roller rink, looking at her now and then, finally coming over when she was alone next to the boards. Making a fast stop and showing his moves.

Stella knowing her friend Liz and the other girls were looking over from the concession stand, whispering and giggling to each other. Made her feel good, lying to him that she was sixteen.

"Well, I been wrong a time or two," he said, "but still, I guess you'd pass for older."

"Older, like how much?" Crinkling her nose — Stella guessed it looked cute like when she practiced it in the mirror — smiling at him, liking the way this Johnny O'Malley was flirting with her, something no boy had done before. Not feeling that unease she often felt around men. Been that way since her real father just walked off, Stella thinking good riddance, happy her mother wouldn't get hit and bruised anymore. Her stepfather, Lester, being made of better stuff, a quiet man working hard for the family. Maybe dull in that way, but at least the man didn't leave those awful bruises on her mother.

Fifteen and Stella wasn't sure what the look meant that Johnny D. O'Malley was putting on her, but she was thinking maybe she wouldn't mind finding out.

"I don't know, let's see . . . eighteen maybe." Johnny grinned, saying, "Guess I ain't saying it right."

"Well, I think you're saying it just fine." She liked the way his cheeks flushed then, yeah, starting to feel easier with him. Not tall, but a nice build and good looking with the blue eyes and wavy hair. Older by a mile, even if she had been eighteen. Stella liking the way Liz was watching from the refreshment stand, talking to some boys, the rest of the girls gone home.

☾

Bennie Dickson had been feeding lines to the pretty blonde, this Stella Mae. Now he was getting caught up in it. Laid it on pretty thick, saying he was a prize fighter in training. That part was true, and Johnny O'Malley was the name he used when he stepped through the ropes.

Not sure why he used the name on her, the name the promotor had come up with, telling Bennie it gave him the Irish edge, a young fighter showing promise, along with a punishing right hook, something they could build on.

Bennie didn't tell her anything about the trouble he'd been in, the stuff he got into back when his old man told him he was acting more loser than winner, anything but a Dickson man. Strike one coming for the stolen car, doing time in that reformatory and shaming the family. Bad Bennie not learning life the easy way, then taking a second swing when he got mixed up in the Missouri bank job, giving up six more hard years in the Missouri pen, same place they kept Pretty Boy Floyd, the place inmates called The Walls on account of that high gray limestone surrounding the place. Life's lessons kicking Bennie hard that time. Working in the prison library and learning to box while inside. Finally convincing the parole board he got the message and wasn't going to make the same mistakes, released into his father's custody. Just turned twenty-six, and Bennie swore to go straight this time.

Might have been partly why he was feeling more Johnny than Bad Bennie right then, telling this girl about the job he just took driving a cab, the money he made allowing him to sweat and work the bag in the Hard Rock gym. Then switching the focus, telling her she skated like a pro.

"You been watching me, huh?"

"Admit I was." From over by the boards, betting all the boys looked her way. From the corner of his eye now, he caught the three mutts eyeing him from over by the food stand, the ones chatting to Stella's friend. The looks meant they guessed who he was and knew about the time he served. Thinking they were better and wanting to prove it. Bennie feeling glad his older brother Spencer had showed up at the rink today, two years older and born on the same day, the two of them of the same blood. Spencer known around town as a tough customer. And although the oldest of the three wasn't there that day, the same went for Darwin, a reputation for watching out for his brothers, likely the main reasons the mutts were keeping their distance. Still, they had that look, like they had something to prove.

(

"Me, *pffft*, nobody sees me. Just a place I meet Liz and the girls and have a few laughs, is all." Stella Mae thinking who had money for roller skating, a nickel just to get in the place, wondering again if Johnny meant what he said, that she looked eighteen, maybe older. Could be on account of the way she'd pulled her hair back that day, not wanting it in her eyes when she skated around, the sweater showing the promise of changes coming, and the ruby lipstick from her mother's dressing table completing the picture. Liked her lips red like that, Stella doing it more these days when her mother was out of the house. Always wiped it off before she went back home.

"How you like it, the music?" Johnny asked. Not sure what the number was piping from the speaker cone. Admitting to her he had a tin ear.

"This one's Lionel Hampton, called 'Hot Mallets.' They play it all the time, everybody skating to it. One the girls like to dance to."

"That right? Well, lucky for Lionel, how about it then, let's see you do it. Dance or skate, either one."

"Just 'cause you say so, huh?" Stella acting indifferent, the smile letting him know she was playing too.

"Just like to watch you move." The blush in his cheeks betrayed him, and he pushed off the boards and skated around the rink, turning and going backwards, moving faster between and around the couples and singles, pretending he was doing it to the music, moving his hips and clowning, looking her way, smiling from across the rink. He swished around and grabbed hold of the boards next to her, saying, "So, come on, girl, catch up if you're any good." And he was off again, going around and looking to see that she was watching. "I've Got a Pocketful of Dreams," coming through the speakers now. The three mutts over at refreshments watching him too.

Standing with a hand against the boards, Stella glanced over at Liz still talking to the boys, likely saying something dumb. Pushing off, she windmilled her arms to gain her balance, half the rink between them.

Johnny coming around and past her, calling out, "Hey, slowpoke."

Picking up speed on the rented skates, she ducked and went under a couple with joined hands, nearly ended on her butt as she bumped them apart. Johnny slowed and let her catch up, holding out his hand, then catching her again from falling, the two of them moving around the rink, holding hands now. Going around two more times, he stopped over by Spencer and introduced her, asking how old Spencer guessed she was, mouthing eighteen behind her back. Also pointed at himself and mouthed to call him Johnny.

Spencer said, "It ain't right to guess a lady's age." Smiling at her, offering his hand.

Stella liking this older brother calling her a lady, told him it was nice to meet him.

Taking her hand again, Bennie did it like it was a natural thing. Stella not pulling away, thinking maybe he did it to keep her from falling, but she liked the way her friend Liz kept looking, the three boys looking too. And she lost track how many times she skated around with him, talking about where they went to school, places around town they both knew. Bennie saying he was serious about his boxing, and driving a cab too. Then asking about her, where she lived, how she liked the school she went to, getting to know her.

Letting him buy her a soda after, the two of them just kept talking, not running out of things. Playing at being eighteen, she pushed away thoughts of her mother worrying about her being out as the afternoon gave way to evening. Then realizing Liz had gone home, Stella told him she'd better get on home too.

"Well, I got my car, can give you a lift if you want?"

Wanting to trust him, but knowing her mother's rule about getting in cars with boys. Saying, "I'm okay, I can walk."

"Well, I'm just offering is all."

They stood talking a few more minutes. Bennie didn't push it, offering to return her skates to the rental desk, asking, "So, how do I see you again?"

"Well, you come next Saturday and maybe you will." Smiling, she let him take the skates.

"Not the brush-off, I hope — I mean, you're gonna show, right?"

"Guess you're gonna find out." Smiling, she started walking, knowing he was watching her, not sure how she'd get another nickel, but she'd get it, and she'd be here next Saturday alright.

. . . two

JUNE 12, 1937

"Handing her a bunch of bull is what you were doing. Showing off and skating around and making me sick. And what kinda fake Paddy name's that, Johnny O'Malley?" The taller one was Randy, leaning against the skate rental desk, blocking Bennie, his two buddies slightly behind and flanking him.

Bennie couldn't recall the last name, but remembered loudmouth Randy as a bully back in grade school, playing it up now for his moron buddies. He reached around and handed in the skates, taking a chance he'd get punched from behind.

The balding guy at the desk looked worried, not wanting any trouble. Bennie thanked him and turned. The three of them closed up and blocked him from moving away and getting to his old Buick. Bennie saying, "Come on, fellas. I don't want trouble."

"Asked you a question. I want an answer, Paddy boy," Randy said, poking a finger at him, three inches taller with maybe twenty pounds on Bennie.

Bennie guessed soft pounds, what the trainer would call a dough boy, likely with a glass chin.

"Something I can smooth out for you fellas?" Coming from behind the three and splitting through them with a shove, Spencer Dickson laid his own skates on the table, paying the old man his three cents, then turning, pressing Randy back, standing nose to nose, about the same size without the dough around his middle. A glance at each of the two morons had them backing off a step.

"Gave that girl a fake name," Randy said, taking a half step back, lining with his buddies, not wanting to meet Spencer's eyes. "Called himself Johnny O'something, like he was playing the big shot. Didn't bother to warn her how he'd done time."

"Guess he left it for some blabbermouth to come along," Spencer said, pushing up his sleeves. "That sound like you, ugly?"

"Hey, I got this, brother." Bennie stepped next to him, knowing what Spencer was doing: shielding his kid brother, just out of the pen and sparing him from getting sent back inside.

"All the fights you get at the club, you can't leave one for me, even an easy one?" Spencer said. "Man, I sure could use a good tune-up." He cranked his neck left to right and got limber, looked from one to the next, all three backing up some more. "But I tell you what, brother, either of these clowns makes a move, they're all yours. Me, I'll feast on this ugly chump." Looking at Randy. "Okay, so you know how this goes, huh?" Spidering his hand on Randy's chest, Spencer shoved him again, making it look easy. "Now you say who you shoving? I say you, ugly. You say who you calling ugly? Tell me I best watch my mouth and quit shoving. And I say I'm shoving you, ugly. What you gonna do about it?" Shoving him again, saying, "Just trying to save all the fuss and cut right to it. That okay with you, ugly?"

Bennie bounced on the toes of his shoes, saying to the moron on the right, "You want to try first?" Looking to the other one. "Or you? Heck, let's save time and all go. All you got to do is put 'em up and start swinging." Egging them on, Bennie tilted his head, giving his chin as a target. Not wanting to get in a fight, knowing it meant a world of trouble, guessing by their looks they didn't like the odds.

"Well, guess she can make up her own mind," Randy said, turning and starting to walk out to his car. "Come on, boys."

"That girl's dirt. Just goes with anybody," the moron on Bennie's right said.

"She go with you?" Bennie said.

"I wouldn't dirty my dick."

Spencer caught Bennie, stopped him from throwing a punch, as Randy tugged his friend by his sleeve.

"You look sideways at my brother again," Spencer said, "and I'm gonna scrape you off my shoe. You understand that?" Watching the three walk the other way.

Then the brothers stepped over to Bennie's wreck, Spencer saying he could use a lift home, adding, "And when're you gonna get yourself a respectable auto? This thing ought to be crushed."

"Can walk if you want to." Bennie clapped his brother's shoulder, led him over to the car and made a show of getting the door for him.

"Just saved your bacon, and you'd make a brother walk home."

"Saved my bacon, hell. Wouldn't break a sweat on those bums."

"Yeah, I know it." Making a fist, Spencer tapped it at his little brother's jaw, knowing the kid showed promise. Just had to stay out of the can long enough to prove it.

Bennie got in and fired up the engine and drove home, back to thinking of Stella Mae Redenbaugh. The girl on the young side, but outside of the shape and blonde hair and blue eyes there was something more to her, different from other girls he'd known. Barely paying attention to the road, he was thinking of driving a cab for a living and doing some honest work for a change. Maybe take his first tip money and look her up, knock on her door and ask her out for a hamburger and Coke. Tell her he couldn't wait till next Saturday.

. . . three

JULY 7, 1937

Released to the family fold back in January, Bennie's sentence commuted by the acting governor. Making good on merit time, he swore to his father he'd find some honest work, get accepted by a college and get back to the books and make something of his life. The foolishness of his youth, walking into that bank, thinking he could take a bag of money and get away with it. Had six years to think on it and turn himself around, telling himself he was never going back to a place like The Walls.

He'd been going with Stella nearly a month now, crazy in love with her, the two of them secretly engaged, waiting till she turned sixteen, then they'd break the news. Things looking up for Bennie Dickson. The cab company offered him steady work, his oldest brother, Darwin, fixing it with the manager, a guy whose sister he'd been dating. Bennie looking to put in some long days running fares, making honest money. The manager giving him a chance, telling him all he needed was to show up for his shifts and get a chauffeur's license.

Bennie getting around to it now before the next shift, driving his clunker down Jackson, finding a parking spot on Eighth, going up the steps of the Topeka City Hall, looking for the Automobile License Bureau, finding it at the far end of the hall, going through a ribbed glass door, the place smelling musty.

The nameplate on the counter told him the clerk was Edward Heidt, a lanky guy with a long neck and a bobbing Adam's apple jiggling when he spoke. His dark hair slicked back, going for the Clark Gable look. Just one woman ahead of Bennie, middle-aged and round, she listened to the Polish joke Edward cracked, the woman telling him she was Lithuanian.

Edward saying, "What's the difference? I mean foreign's foreign, ain't it?" Stamping a form, taking her fee, counting out her change.

The woman rolled her eyes at Bennie as she left, looked like she was happy to get out of there.

Bennie nodded to her, then stepped to the counter.

Edward said, "Wonder how you say that's a nice wide beam in Polack?"

"Lithuanian."

Looking up, Edward said, "Yeah, immigrants, huh? Third one in a week, can hardly talk American, think they'd learn it, huh?"

"You mean English," Bennie said, then almost wished he hadn't.

Dumb eyes clouding, Edward looked at him, rose up — a few inches on Bennie — and said, "You a wiseacre, huh?"

"Meant nothing by it."

"And where're you from? I seen you before?"

"From right here, and maybe you've seen me. Town's not so big."

"And I guess you heard the one about the bigger the dog, the harder the bite?"

"Yeah, a good old cliché." Bennie smiled, trying to keep it friendly.

"Sounding more French."

"Means it's an old chestnut, about the harder the bite. Look, I just need my license upgraded, pal." Bennie put the filled-out form down and slid it across.

"That's it, huh, all a wiseacre needs?"

"Like I said, I meant nothing by it."

Glancing over the form, Edward stopped on Bennie's name. "Well, I'll be." His eyes lit, and he pointed a finger at him. "Bennie Dickson, sure, that's where I know you. Read all about you. Robbed a bank or something, wasn't it? Yeah, saw your mug in the paper, about getting pardoned by the governor himself. How you mended your ways, found your way back to society, and here you are." Now he was beaming. "Bet you make your folks proud, huh?"

"Best we leave them out of it." Bennie smiled, but felt his cheeks flushing. "How about you take your stamp," glancing to the nameplate, "Edward, and you plant one right there," pointing to the form, "tell me what I owe, and I'll be out of your hair." Glancing at the Clark Gable do.

"Now I got a jailbird telling me my job." Turning his head like there was somebody at the far end of the room, Edward pointed to the nameplate with the job title under it, saying, "You got any idea what it means?"

"Yeah, means you're the clerk, guy who stamps papers and collects a fee."

"The guy who can find a hundred reasons to say uh uhn, no way. Guy who can make you wait or even come back. Starting to get who I am?"

"Sure, had you pegged right off, the guy who gets kicks talking down to immigrants, ones coming here for a better life. Sure, I know you, I met all kinds of you, and you ask me, your kind stinks." Hands planted on the counter, Bennie gave the stare back.

"Well, there we go, guess you told me, huh? Now, let's see, a chauffeur's license, *hmm*, another French word for you. Okay, you go on and step right in line, let me look this over. Make sure you got the i's dotted."

"Except there's no line." Bennie took a deep breath.

"Well then, how about you go and make one. And if you can't find it, you just wait, there'll be one soon enough, then you get right in back of it. Give you time to cool off. Then we'll see what happens."

"Okay, I guess you're a funny man, Edward, or you go by Eddie?" Bennie reeled in his temper, flicked his fingers against the nameplate. "And for what it's worth, maybe we got off on the wrong foot. Now, how about it, huh? I got a job same as you, one I got to get to."

"Yuh, I understand that, need me to upgrade your license."

Bennie kept the tight smile, but felt his temper winning out.

"Next." Edward looked past him like there was a line behind him, Adam's apple bobbing.

"Look, you made your point, okay, Edward?" Trying one more time, Bennie pushed the form forward, saying, "And I'm sorry we got off wrong. Now, how about it, huh?"

Ignoring him, Edward Heidt took a stack of papers, lifted his stamp and hit a couple pages, re-sorted them into a neat stack to his right.

"Just gonna stand there stamping your dumb papers, like I'm not here, huh?"

Pursing his lips, Edward gave a soft whistle, not looking up.

"One more time, Eddie. I need you to . . . ah, to hell with it." Bennie's temper washed over the dam, coming in a rush. And before he could rein it in, he popped the guy in his puckered mouth, not a full blow, but enough to stop Edward from whistling. What followed was almost worth it, looking at the dumb, surprised look, blood leaking past Edward's lips.

Edward put a couple fingers to his numb mouth. "You rotten son of a bitch, you hit me." Looking at the blood. "You, you . . ."

"You know what, Edward, how about I come back when you're not so busy? Can see you got some mopping up to do." Bennie took his form and turned to go, thinking he'd explain things to the manager at work, sure he could smooth things out about the license. Maybe come back when someone less cranky was working the counter. And he was halfway to the door.

Edward flung the stack of bloodied papers over his head, eyes wild, and jumped up on the counter — more agile than he looked — and he leapt across, giving an animal yell midair, bulldogging Bennie to the floor.

Rolling free of him, Bennie was quick to his feet, let the taller man get up, seeing the roundhouse coming from a mile. Ducking it, Bennie stepped in and chopped a quick combination into the ribs. Edward reeling back and folding up, tried getting his breath back. Then he threw his arms wide and came in for a grab, trying to turn it into a wrestling match, ripping the collar half off Bennie's shirt. Hooking a short right to Edward's ear, Bennie nailed him with a left uppercut to the chin, then feinted, and landed a straight right that sent the clerk back to the floor. Bennie asking, "Now I knocked some sense in you, how about you go get your stamp?"

"You hit me . . . *ahhh!*" Edward got his legs under him again and charged in swinging, looked like he was trying to fly. And Bennie pummeled him with a half dozen body blows. Left Edward Heidt curled on the floor with his hands over his head. The papers all over the place.

Taking his bad temper with him, Bennie left, cursing down the hall, shoes clanking on the polished floor, asking himself what the hell he was thinking, walking out to his car, guessing cab driving wasn't going to fit into his future plans after all.

. . . *four*

JULY 7, 1937

"Your hand, what happened?" Stella's mother ushered him into the front room. Calling him Johnny and telling him to call her Hattie.

"Well, you see, guess Stella told you I'm a boxer, ma'am. Hazards of getting in the ring, I guess." Bennie stood on the rug while she inspected his hand, told him he should get ice on it. And he liked her straight off, expecting her to react like: what was a guy in his mid-twenties doing calling on her teenage girl. Instead of shaking her head, she shook his hand, concerned about his swollen and scraped knuckles.

"It's really nothing, ma'am. Guess you get used to it, sparring a couple times a week. Tell you the truth, I just didn't take much notice." He looked around the place, had a nice homey feel, and he told her so. He'd wondered on the drive over here whether Hattie would insist on coming along as a chaperone, again thinking of the difference in age.

"A boxer, that like a prize fighter? And it's Hattie."

"That's right, Hattie. They call me a middleweight."

"Middleweight, that so? Are you any good? Oh, you must be."

"Well, without crowing about it, Pops, my trainer, told me if I stick to it and work hard, I could end up the next Jack Dempsey, the one they call the Manassa Mauler, some call him Kid Blackie, maybe you heard of him?" Looking hopeful, but seeing the name didn't mean anything, he went on saying, "Anyway, Pops figures I could work on a near all-action style, take no prisoners and punch like dynamite. Tells me all the time I got a fair left hook. Don't mean to sound big-headed about it, ma'am." Thinking he was putting on a pretty good show, not feeling like an up-an-comer after decking the guy at the license office.

"I guess that's all good." Hattie smiled, leading him into the parlor, saying, "Except you call me ma'am again, you're gonna have to defend yourself, put 'em up, right in my front room." Winking, she pointed for him to sit, the blue sofa and matching chairs with needlepoint cushions, the photos of Stella and her brother, Alvie, up on the mantle, some when they were just kids, some when they were in school.

"Thank you, Hattie." Smiling at her, he felt right at home, sitting in one of the chairs, not wanting to lean back on the needlepoint pillow, didn't want to change its shape, the view out the window giving him a glance at his old wreck out by the curb, could see up and down the street in case the cops came for him. "Real nice place you got, and close to the college too."

"Where I'm hoping Stella'll be in a year or so." Sitting across from him, Hattie asked about his own schooling.

"Well, my father wants me to enroll at Washburn and study some law."

"So, the prizefighting's just in the meantime?" Hattie

looked hopeful, smoothing her skirt and sitting on the settee across from him. Offering him tea.

"Another time, ma— There I go again. Hattie. And yes, I suppose the boxing's in the meantime, but who ever knows where things take you, am I right?"

"Couldn't agree more, Johnny. And I'd love to hear more about you making a future for yourself."

"Well, aside from working on my record, the boxing I mean, winning some purses and moving up the ranks, my overall plan's to hit the law books, earn that degree and get myself appointed to the bar. And if the old cabbage doesn't get too rattled from prize fighting," looking down at his skinned knuckles, "then maybe I'll defend some cases. Funny, Jack Dempsey, the champ I told you about, he figures it the same way, win a couple titles, then hang up the gloves, maybe do some stunt work and put on boxing exhibitions, then settle and practice the law."

"Well, guess it's good to have a couple irons in the fire."

"I guess so too, Hattie." Bennie grinned. "Another idea's to get out to Hollywoodland and do some stunt work while Stella does some acting like she's been talking about. Hope she told you that."

"Oh, that girl's bursting with ideas too. Acting and singing, anything with a spotlight, but I guess it's all a good thing." She leaned close and lowered her voice. "And I tell you, Johnny, she gets a notion, then best step out of the way, or get your toes tromped on, you get the picture." Hattie smiled like she was proud. "Almost sounds like you two are cut from the same swatch. A boxing lawyer and a singing movie star, sounds like you two got it made."

And he wasn't sure why, but he told her he liked reading and writing poetry too.

"You don't say?" Hattie brightened, saying she was partial to a little Lord Byron, and Keats and Shelley.

"Some of my favorites too. And there's William Ernest Henley, you know him? One who wrote 'Invictus.' Another favorite of mine."

She admitted she didn't, and he recited a few lines about the night that covered, black as a pit, about being the master of his fate and the captain of his soul.

Hattie said she enjoyed talking to him and getting to know him, asking if he was sure about the tea.

"Next time'd be nice, Hattie." He got to his feet, hearing Stella coming down the hall, turning to her as she entered the room. "Well, don't you look nice, Stella Mae."

"That a question or you saying it?" Smiling at him, Stella offered her hand instead of throwing herself in his arms and planting a kiss, acting shy with her mother looking on. Saying, "Sorry to keep you, Johnny, but this hair, I swear, I'm gonna chop it like rhubarb." Laughing about it, seeing his hand all red and swollen, not asking what happened with her mother looking on. Instead, asking if he was all set, taking his unhurt hand, Stella was tugging him for the door.

Following to the door, Hattie wished them a good time, asking what time Stella would be home.

"Anytime you say, Hattie," Bennie said, thinking he wouldn't mind too much if she did come along as chaperone. As much as he wanted to spend time with Stella, he enjoyed talking to her mother, thinking that girls were younger versions of the mother. Pretty happy about that.

"How's uh . . . say nine thirty, or let's make it ten. That alright with you, Johnny?"

"I'll have her home right on the bell," Bennie said, smiling again, saying it was a real pleasure to meet her, saying again she had a swell house, and offering his hand.

Going ahead of Stella, he got the car door, letting Stella in. Shutting it, he went around and gave a wave to the house and got behind the wheel. Glad the old heap started up without him having to get out and prop up the hood.

"Imagine asking what time to have your fiancée home." Stella grinned at him, sliding her hand on his thigh, her mother waving from the door.

"Guess she hasn't worked out that part yet." He glanced to the house, letting the engine warm up a bit, praying for it not to backfire.

"You kidding, Momma'd have a kitten. And what was that bull you were feeding her?"

"What bull?"

"I don't know, sounded like a poem."

"Exactly what it was. William Ernest Henley, a few lines from 'Invictus.' Claimed she liked it, so I recited some."

"Never tried that on me."

"Didn't know you cared for it."

"Don't know everything about me, do you?"

"Guess not, but I plan to find out."

"Well, you can start by telling me what happened to your hand, just the minute you drive from this curb." Smiling at him, turning and waving to the house.

"There you go, talking like a wife." Wanting to kiss her, but waiting till they were down the block, waving again to Hattie by the door. Guessing the engine was warm enough, pulling from the curb. Couldn't wait to get Stella Mae alone.

☾

The kind of a kiss to remember. Stella Mae not acting like any sixteen-year-old, Bennie having a hard time keeping his hands on the wheel, taking her for a drive out to Lake

Shawnee, trying to find a way to tell her his real name wasn't Johnny O'Malley. Started to say so a couple of times, but she wasn't giving him a chance.

The two of them ended up doing more parking than driving, a quiet spot by the beach. Stella crowding him behind the wheel, getting up in his lap and facing him, eager to show him things, pulling the shawl blouse over her head, saying it was okay since they were practically married. Naked from the waist up, she surprised him with the things she knew.

After the parking, they straightened their clothes, and he got the engine to cough back to life. He drove to an eatery called Dover's Hall, and they sat in a corner booth and talked over hamburgers and Cokes. Holding her hand, he still couldn't get himself to tell her he was Bennie, not Johnny. He did ease into telling her about the time he served in the reformatory for swiping a car, but kept the bank robbing and the time he served in the state pen for another time. Revisiting his past, one mistake at a time.

"So, you're a little bit car thief, a little bit boxer, and poetry's what, like a smoke screen?"

"A smoke screen?"

"Meaning like you were being all polite, telling a poem to my momma. And sometimes you treat me like I might break." She put her mouth on the straw and sipped, having fun with him.

"Well, I turned Boy Scout when I was seven, still got the badges to show for it. Spencer too. Two of us used to go around doing deeds. Some habits are hard to break, I guess."

"A do-gooder turned car thief." She grinned like she wasn't buying what he was shoveling.

"Well, fact is, me and Spence one time saved this woman trying to drown herself at the local pond, water dark as tea. Made the front page of most of the Kansas papers, the governor proposing me and Spence for the Carnegie Medal."

"You're pulling my leg."

"Not yet I'm not." Putting his hand on her knee under the table.

"You saved a suiciding woman, then turned around and landed in a reformatory. What do you call that?"

"A mixed-up kid."

"Told my ma you're gonna be a lawyer, getting her to like you."

"Want me to tell you one, a poem, get you to like me too?" Bennie slid close on the bench seat.

"Already hooked me, you dummy. And easy on the onions." Reaching for his burger and pulling the onion slice out, dropping it on his plate. "Okay, go on, tell me one." She leaned in, looking in his eyes.

And he recited "She Walks in Beauty." Saying the lines of beauty walking like the night, cloudless climes and starry nights, and all that's best of dark and bright. Telling her it was by Lord Byron, then leaning in for a kiss.

Putting up a finger to stop him. "Well, you're one fine smoothie, you are. Words are beautiful, but, oh man, those onions . . ."

"You want to hear more or not?"

She slid a couple feet away, saying, "Okay, go ahead."

Saying this one was by Keats, he recited "Bright Star" about her tender-taken breath, and the soft fall and swell, and the sweet unrest, and swooning to death.

"Not sure what it means, but it's something."

"Saying you like it?"

"I like the way you said it. You got any more?"

"Yeah, even some of my own, but how about I save them for special."

"So, you recite those on account of me knocking your socks off?"

"Maybe." Getting close again, whispering, "How about we get back in the car?"

Stella not pulling away or pretending she didn't know what he was after, asked the waitress for Life Savers, letting him walk her back to the car, him opening the door for her. Sliding her hand around back of his head as he tried to crank the engine, she called his hair wavy and told him his eyes were nice. Bennie peeling the Five Flavor pack, picking lime, Stella going for cherry. Guessing the sadness wasn't showing in his nice eyes, he knew what he had to do. Knowing he was leaving right after he drove her home.

Another kiss to remember, and he dropped her off right at ten, then drove to his family's home on West Fourteenth Street. Coming around the corner, he saw the patrol car from halfway up the block, parked by the curb. Nobody inside, meaning the cop was inside talking to his folks. Likely wanting to arrest him for what happened at the license office. Not likely to take the word of an ex-con when he said it was in self-defense.

Backing up the old wreck, Bennie took the next street and parked in the lane. He got out and went along the Nelsons' hedgerow, ducking through the backyards, hoping the neighbor's dog was inside the house. Waiting until the cop came out of the front door, Bennie going to the back door, listening to be sure Spencer was out, then he tiptoed up the stairs, his parents still out front talking to the cop, could hear the murmur of their voices.

Grabbing extra pants and borrowing a couple of Spencer's shirts, he folded them into a paper bag, took the money he kept in the drawer and slipped back down. His mother clanging in the kitchen now, the smell of his father's pipe coming from the front room, the old man seeing the cop out, and sounding miserable. Easing out the back door, Bennie went back through the yards and to his car. It hurt to leave his family and Stella Mae, but if he stayed he'd be facing felony charges, and there was no way he was going back to The Walls just for punching some jerk at the license office.

Driving into the coming dark, not sure yet where he was going, thinking maybe Kansas City. Had some friends there who hung out late at the Lido Club. Maybe they'd put him up for a couple of nights till he figured things out.

...*five*

The hurt was big, but the anger was bigger. Stella making up her mind to get on with her life, telling herself to forget about Bennie Dickson or Johnny D. O'Malley, or whatever he was calling himself. Taking off without a word, and the cops coming around her mother's house and asking questions, saying Ben Dickson had done six in the pen, released just months before he met her at the roller rink. And now he was a wanted man for an unprovoked assault on a clerk at the motor vehicle office. The officers calling him a dangerous individual. "A good potato'll rot next to a bad one," one of them warned her mother.

Johnny had said he wanted to see more of her, Stella telling him he could see all he wanted, making that plain enough in back of his old car by the lake. The two of them secretly engaged, waiting till she turned of age. What did that even mean, secretly engaged. He said he wanted things to be proper. Nothing proper about lying, then running off and leaving her.

Not seeing him at the roller rink that afternoon back in July, Stella came home and was questioned by the law, then spent the evening answering more questions from her mother, being forbidden to see him again. The folding of her arms meant she was dead serious about it. All the while Stella sat with her own arms folded, biting her lip, staring at the telephone like a fool, practically had to force herself to breathe. Wanting to throw the contraption out the door for not ringing, she guessed she wouldn't give old Bennie Dickson or whatever he was calling himself the time of day if he did call. Told herself she was done with him. Maybe done with all men, nothing but a bunch of liars, same as her father had been.

☾

"All part of growing up," her mother finally said when she calmed down — took better than a week — sitting next to her in the parlor, putting an arm around her daughter. "But you heard what the policeman said about that boy stealing cars and robbing banks and going around hurting people. Good Lord."

"You liked him fine yourself, going on about him reciting poetry."

"Well, I guess he threw dust in my eyes, same as you. Point is, you're a teenage girl changing in body and mind, and I'm guessing some things are slower than others catching up. I blame myself, not you. Should have known better than letting him take you for that drive."

"How am I gonna catch up if you keep telling me slow down? Some things I just got to find out for myself, and bump into a few things."

"Well, maybe that's true, but I worry about the bumping part, and it's best you just slow down and aim to be a better judge of character. And this Johnny or Bennie or whatever, he's a full-grown man, showing you what he wants you to see. And like all men, you get right down to it, they're just after the one thing."

"Mother!" Stella pretended her shock, smiling and seeing her mother soften.

"It's the God's truth, they can't help it." Sending a play-elbow at her daughter.

"That go for Lester?" Stella giggled, giving the elbow back.

"Heavens, no. Your stepfather's a one-in-a-million man, and I think you know that, providing for us all these years."

"Yeah, I know it."

"Man's never given a word of complaint about it. You just wait and take it slow, then you go and find yourself a good Lester."

"I remember Daddy hitting you. Seen him do it and it sent me hiding under the bed, figured me and Alvie were next."

"Well, Miss Grown-Up, you know we don't talk about that runaway man. So, how about you go and sweep out the parlor, and take your mind off that Bennie or Johnny what's-his-name? Oh, before you do, be a dear and run down to Grainger's and fetch a sack of flour."

Started to object, then she nodded and sighed. "You want the cotton sack, ones you give to the Endicotts?"

"The Roller Mills, you know the one."

Stella knew her mother gave the sacks to Mrs. Endicott, who made them into diapers for her baby twins, helping her out a little.

Her mother saying, "The flour's for those cookies you like, the jammies."

"*Mmm mmm*, I'm going."

"There's a dollar in my purse. And make sure Emmett gives you the right change, not that I don't trust him. Man's just got his mind elsewhere, fishing or checkers or some such thing."

Stella thinking it beat hanging around, catching more of her mother's told-you-sos. Taking the dollar and going out the door, she heard her mother calling for her to stop and pick up the mail.

Stella calling back how she had to do everything around here. Glad things were right between her and her mother again.

(

Nearly dropped the flour sack at the post office wicket, staring at the letter with her name on it, no return but knowing it was from him, postmarked Chicago. Her heart jumped in her throat as she tore into it. Standing in the corner with the ten-pound sack between her feet, reading the lines.

First words were sorry he had to jump like that, turned out the father of the guy at the license office, one Earl Heidt, carried some sway in this town. And old man Heidt was insisting on charges of assault with intent to kill, and the cops were going along. The letter promised he'd smooth things out, just not sure how yet. Meantime he was staying with a couple of aunts, going from one to the other, asking Stella to stay mum about it. Not sure when he could come back, not sure where he was going next, but told her he was holding her in his heart, and swore they'd be together soon. Said he'd write again when he could. And signed it Johnny.

And even with the fake name at the end of it, the hurt and anger lifted like fog, and in spite of the ten pounds of flour, Stella skipped out of there, down the steps and danced the sack down Fourteenth Street, with no idea of what lay ahead.

. . . *six*

MAY 5, 1938

Sitting with one foot up on the crate he used like a coffee table, Bennie flipped open the cylinder of the .38 Smith & Wesson, the one he stole from the Peerless Laundry. He thumbed the hammer, the stock feeling good in his hand. And he liked the four-inch barrel, this one firing high-pressure loads like a lawman's gun, designed to fire clean through a car's body. Robbed the laundry twice and got enough cash both times to last a few months. Took a dandy silver pocket watch from the manager's desk drawer the second time too. A Swiss one with the small hand and dial, kept pretty good time as long as he remembered to wind it.

When he started back into robbing, he got this feeling like he wanted to fight something, but most of the time he wasn't sure what it was he wanted to hit. Maybe that was just in his nature. Along with breaking into the Peerless place twice, there had been a half dozen other places he hit since coming to Tinseltown. Mostly lightweight stuff, breaking in after hours. With no relations, no friends and no steady work to be found, he took care of himself the only way he knew. Not like it made up for it, but he used some of the stolen cash to register under the name of Johnny D. O'Malley at the university, enrolled to study English and physics, set on getting his life in order. The one thing his father would agree with, being a chemistry teacher at Topeka High, wanting to be proud of his son.

And Bennie was back to boxing as Johnny O'Malley, same as he did up in Illinois after leaving Kansas, winning every bout and showing that promise his trainer, Pop, had talked about. His last one was stopped halfway through the second, Johnny O'Malley mauling some Mexican kid from Chavez Ravine, the kid calling himself Puncho. Bennie stepped under the rope and pictured the kid as Edward Heidt from the license bureau, the reason he had to go on the lam. Just went straight at Puncho and didn't stop hitting him till the ref stepped in and pulled him off, raising his hand in the air.

Bennie smiled now, thinking all he had to do was picture every opponent as Edward Heidt, could be enough to carry him to the welterweight crown.

Snapping the cylinder with a wag of his hand, he set the revolver by the tin platter of penny candy. Getting an idea that he'd write to Stella again, tell her how he set out the platter of Life Savers every day, kept it right in plain sight, keeping himself from the itch of diving in and eating the green ones first, not allowing himself to do it while he was in training. He'd call it his idea of discipline, guessing it would make her laugh. Tell her he kept them handy for the times he had a hamburger with onion.

Checking his new watch, he gave himself a half hour to write the letter before going to Duffey's and skipping rope and working the heavy bag, maybe don the head gear and get in a few rounds of sparring, see if Duffey had lined up another fight. After the KO of Puncho there ought to be more coming his way, maybe even one with a purse. Reaching for the paper and pen, he scratched her name, picked out a couple of green ones and started chewing, writing the opening lines from "Invictus," telling her it was his favorite at the moment. Reminding her about "I've Got a Pocketful of Dreams," calling it their song, said he had it playing right then as he wrote. Humming it as he chewed, he scratched that it made him think of her. Wondered if that sounded corny, absently picking out another green one.

☾

The folded money dropped out from the letter. Bennie writing to her again — Stella banding the eight months of letters together, Bennie sending one a week — Stella hiding them under her mattress. He said the fifteen dollars would cover the fare for the Super Chief, plus he tucked in some extra for meals. Told her she could get on in Newton, and it would take her right into Los Angeles, where he'd pick her up at the station. Said he couldn't wait and had it all worked out. That is, if she still wanted to join him. Signed it Johnny.

Not yet sixteen, Stella was thinking of that question he wanted to ask, the most important one of his life. Wondering if he'd get around to telling her his real name before getting down on one knee. Stella's heart was jumping, thoughts of getting out of her mother's house, getting married and keeping her own house. Nothing against her mother or Lester, she loved them both to bits, her brother, Alvie, too, but after her horrible troubles of late, she just wanted to go.

Live out where they made pictures, and maybe end up on that silver screen, singing and dancing like Ginger Rogers in *Stage Door*. Any young girl's dream. And down the road there'd be a couple of kids playing in the yard. Hadn't imagined it happening so fast, falling in love with a guy wanting to ask the most important question of his life. And there it was, her way out of Kansas, this place that had become nothing but dried-up, where everything was the color of sand.

There'd been nothing for her here since the day she went with Liz and took that ride home from the man at the roller rink, happened on Halloween. At first thinking it was somebody they knew, finding out different once they got in the car and the man was driving off, but guessing it was safe enough with two of them there. Dropping Liz at her house, and instead of driving the extra three blocks, the man turned the car around and drove Stella out of town, parked and tore at her clothes, punching her unconscious and when he was done, ended up tossing her from the car.

She couldn't hide it from her mother. Her mother crying with her, then practically had to drag her to the doctor. Finding out she had gonorrhea and needing those horrible treatments. Wasn't long and the whole town knew about it, and her life became the worst kind of hell. Everybody at school treating her like she had pox, same at the roller rink, even Liz kept her distance, just talked to her on the phone and didn't want to be seen with her. Stella wanted to write Johnny about it, tell him to come back and find that son of a bitch and beat him up. Or maybe worse.

But now she was leaving all that behind. Swaying down the streets of Topeka with the old suitcase in her hand, singing that Louis Armstrong number. Wanted to surprise him and sing it for him. It didn't matter old lady Endicott was watching from her porch. Let her look, let them all look and think there goes loose-legs Stella Mae; she's gone crazy. The clap finally taking her mind, touch her and you might get crotch crickets. She'd heard it all, most of it in whispers behind her back.

Buying the ticket with the money he sent, first time riding on a train, Stella looked out the window and watched the farms and towns flash by and disappear behind her. "Santa Fe all the way" was what the banner read at the station house. The coach car swaying and rocking her as the Super Chief, dubbed the train of the stars, rolled westward. Newton to Dodge City to La Junta, then through New Mexico and Arizona, places she'd only heard or read about. Looking out the window at the new sights, with a new life waiting for her.

When she could take her eyes from the window, she asked the conductor for paper and pen and started to write him some poems. After a few tries she just ended writing the name Stella Mae Dickson, liked the way the D swooped. And thinking she should drop the Mae, guessing it sounded too Kansas. The land out the window going from dead to green, and then she was seeing California out the window: Needles and Barstow and San Bernardino and on into Pasadena, the landscape going from cows to concrete to culture.

. . . seven

MAY 20, 1938

The porter pulled back the coach door, and Stella breathed that warm California air, looking out at La Grand, over the men in their hats and the couples waiting on the arriving passengers. Offering his hand, the porter told her to watch her step and thanked her for riding the Atchison, Topeka and Santa Fe. Stella joked about the name being as long as the ride; the old man smiled yellowed teeth at the same line he'd heard about a hundred times. Told her that was a good one.

Looking along the platform, she spotted Bennie jumping up and down in the throng, and he saw her too, looked like he was swimming through the folks. And she pressed her way to him, dropped the shabby suitcase at her feet and threw her arms around him and kissed him a long time. Calling him Johnny, thinking it suited him more than Bennie.

"Well, Stella Mae, just look at you." Lifting her in his arms and swinging her around, admiring her. "Ain't you a sight."

"Well, sure I am. Been nearly two days sitting in the same clothes, you just set me down and take me where I can get cleaned up and wash this mop of hair, then you're gonna really see something."

"Yeah, just bet I will." He set her down and she fell back into his arms and kissed him some more, Bennie tasting like Life Savers. Didn't matter people were looking.

Taking her suitcase, Bennie told her he just rented them a place, leading her to the parking lot. "A house, and wait'll you see it. Bigger than my folks' place, yours too. Got a fireplace in the front room, *ooh wee*, you're not gonna believe it."

"Why'd we need that? It's boiling." Looking past the station, everything lush and wonderful and warm.

"Cools down at night like you're gonna see." Weaving and angling through the bodies milling along the platform, he dropped her suitcase in the trunk of the Packard, the one he stole for the occasion, driving along Wilshire Boulevard, talking some about the new car, and showing her the sights. Drove past the colonnade of Metro-Goldwyn-Mayer, stopping at a drive-in soda fountain, telling her it was his favorite place. The first time she'd ever had a sundae. She told him it was pretty good. Then he took her past the first drive-in theatre she ever laid eyes on, Stella having never seen anything like it. Sit in your car and see a picture on the world's biggest screen. Man, she was loving this place already.

Bennie talking like a born Angeleno, pointing out the San Gabriel Mountains, telling her about the L.A. River flood they had earlier in the year, driving through the hustle of downtown, the tallest buildings Stella had ever seen, the bustle in the streets, people and cars going every which way, red streetcars and yellow coaches and all kinds of cars and trucks. Bennie winding his way to the rented house that took most of the cash he had left from the Peerless Laundry jobs, enough to cover a couple months' rent the owner demanded up front.

Stella cranked down the window, put her head out and looked up at the palm trees.

"Yeah, ain't they something. Grow out here like musk thistle." Then he was telling her he had a fight coming up. Just a club fight, but he wanted her to come and see his stuff, called her his lucky charm. Telling her about the Puncho knockout.

"Don't know you need the luck, you sound pretty sure. And don't know if I could stomach seeing you get your head knocked around."

"Don't think you're paying attention, lady. Not how it works when I step in those ropes. See, it's gonna be me doing the head knocking. The bum they got me with's . . . well, forget his name, but my trainer's thinking it won't go three rounds before he's lights out and kissing the canvas, and you can bank on that."

"Well, you do sound pretty sure."

"Been talking to this promotor, Jacobs, wants me going by Johnny O'Mallet. Figures if I work hard, someday I'll be headlining at the Olympic." Looking at her like that should mean something.

"Hard to keep you two straight. Johnny one minute, Bennie the next, huh?" Grinning at him, fanning a hand at herself.

He was quiet a moment, then said, "Yeah, well, I was set to tell you next time I saw you, see, I had a fight lined up back home that day I met you at the rink, and I was feeling more Johnny than Bennie. It's the name when I get in the ring, see? Makes me feel like I'm winning. Never got the right chance to say my real one before I had to hightail it. Talk about getting off on the wrong foot, huh?"

"Topped it by getting yourself wanted for assault with intent to kill. The cops coming knocking on my door and my mother nearly having a kitten. Should've seen the look on her face." Stella laughed about it now.

"Well, I'm sure sorry about it, a heck of a mess. One I'm gonna straighten out. I like your mother, really do, and I don't want her thinking bad of me. Hey, you're making fun of me, huh?" Seeing her laughing into her fist.

"Well, sure I am. None of that matters now, does it? I'm just happy being here. Look at all these palm trees." Tipping her head up, watching a line of them whizzing by. Saying, "Just you and me, Johnny, starting out clean and making a life." She slid over, leaned across and kissed him again.

"God bless me and my one-in-a-million girl. That's what you are." Slinging his arm around her, one hand on the wheel of the Packard, he drove to the bungalow he rented, pulling around the back, saying, "Well, here it is, our good start. And you can bet I got ideas and I'm going places too. Bennie the lawyer and Johnny the fighter, and you're going to see." Telling her he had a thought while waiting on the train, how he planned to get rich and keep it that way. "You believe it?"

"Think I'd believe just about anything you say." Stepping to the porch and going through the door of the place, Stella was taking it in, already thinking about where to put the furniture. Not much of it in the place: just an armchair in front of a fireplace, an orange crate in front of it with a dish of candy. Could see a mattress in the back room and the place had a sparse look, but it was clean. And she loved it.

"Well, first things first . . ." Going to a knee in front of her, his voice echoing in the near-empty place, he slid a hand in a pocket, taking out a small box, asking how she'd like to be Mrs. Bennie Dickson.

She drew her breath and felt her heart drum. Looking at the ring, then letting him slip it on her finger. "Sure takes a lot of getting used to, being your girl, Bennie Dickson."

"If that's a good thing, then guess I can take that as a yes?" Bennie looked hopeful, still down on one knee in front of the brick fireplace.

"Didn't come all this way to say no." Dropping on him, Bennie losing his balance, and both of them tumbling on the floor, in front of the hearth.

"Didn't figure I'd ask straight off, huh?" On the floor, looking at her.

"Well, knew you had something to ask, your letter said the most important question of your life. And guess I didn't figure you sent all that money for me to come this far so you could take me roller skating. But, yeah, I'm kinda surprised." Stella held her hand straight out past his head, saying she loved the ring, and she loved him too. Then looked serious, asking, "They got roller skating here?"

"They got everything here."

And they were kissing again, Bennie saying he ought to bundle her up and carry her to the bedroom, then saying, "Or, maybe best we wait. I want to do this right."

"You want to wait? What exactly am I missing, already did it that time in the car." Tipping her head back, looking in his eyes.

"Yeah, but that was Kansas, this is California. We do things different here."

"You saying it's better here?" Rolling on her back on the wood floor.

"Lady, everything's better here. Bigger too. But what I'm saying's maybe we should hold off, you know . . ."

Holding up her hand and studying the ring. "Well, you want to get all church-going about it, Bennie Dickson, then

I say wait if you want. Just, in the meantime, and if you don't mind, I'll go make some time with Johnny O'Malley. See what he says about it."

"Makes you think he'd say different?"

"Call it a hunch." One more look at the ring, a little big on her finger, she'd have to be careful not to lose it, sliding her hand down and along his side, then kissing him long and hard. Guessed she could confess her own lies, how she wasn't sixteen yet — not old enough to marry, 'less she got permission from her folks, that or lied about it at city hall — and there was the rest of what had happened to her, knowing she'd keep that part to herself, bury it deep inside.

. . . eight

MAY 21, 1938

Lying on the mattress in the back room, looking at her, he told her she had the warmest, smoothest skin on a girl, then he was back to talking about stepping back in the ring and making easy money. "Punching my way through school and ending up being a lawyer."

"How about getting hurt?"

"The trick's to do the hurting, not the getting hurt." Calling himself a welterweight, six-and-oh fighting out of the Spartan Club in Chi-town, four-and-one since coming to the coast. Told her about the Brown Bomber and Sixto Escobar and Max Schmeling, the kind of purses the top guys made. Bennie figuring on training hard and working his way up.

She put a finger to his lip, saying, "*Shh.*"

"Just don't want you to worry."

"Not so much that I worry, because I bet you're good at it. It's just, don't you ever talk about, you know, something else?" Giving him a sweet smile. "You know I'm a girl, right?"

"Can tell you about my law books."

"If you want to put me to sleep. Not why I figured we got in this bed."

"Can tell you I want to take you to the courthouse, have the police judge marry us straight off." Sliding his hand below the blanket, running it along her smooth back.

"Now you're talking."

He propped the pillow behind his neck, saying, "I got another idea, how we can make easy money. Get our life on the fast track."

"Got a feeling we're not talking about boxing trophies and law degrees."

"Well, school's gonna cost money, and until I get that degree, we're gonna need some cash."

"Well, I'm not broken, I can work."

"You hear of Bonnie and Clyde?"

"Bank robbers that ended in bloody bits, sure. Remember that awful photo. Tell me you're not thinking . . . oh, my God." And she was laughing.

"What's funny about it?"

"Nothing funny about getting shot, just, come on . . . you're pulling my leg again, right?"

He laid his head back on the pillow, looking at the ceiling.

"Well, I just can't see me walking in no bank, fifteen years old and yelling get your hands up and scaring folks out of their wits. Never even held a gun." She remembered reading about the Barrows speeding along those Louisiana piney woods, Bonnie next to Clyde in a car going over eighty, driving straight into that ambush. Clyde shot in the head. Stella thinking of Bonnie seeing him die and screaming as the half dozen state cops kept shooting and got her too. "Besides, who'd believe me?"

"You just say fifteen?"

She shrugged, saying, "What's three months?"

"Guess we're both just a pair of liars." He smiled. "Me Johnny, and you sixteen."

"So, how do you do it?"

"Not much to it really, you go in and you point a gun. Doesn't matter about your age. But if we're not of the same mind, I won't mention it again, just put it right out of my head. Find a new way to go."

"Just a lot to take in. One minute you're making an honest woman of me, next one you got me robbing a bank."

"Well, maybe so, but the way I figure it, a man with a wife's got to have ambition."

"And I can see you got plenty of it, boxing your way through law school, but, come on, just look how they ended up, those two." Still thinking he might be joking with her. "I mean, you've run into trouble and paid the price . . ."

"Actually, more of it than I told you." Telling her he did six years for the Missouri bank job. "Learned from my mistakes, and I learned from some of the pros in the joint too."

"Pros who got arrested."

"See, the way I see it, old Clyde got a couple things right. One thing, he was a V8 man, figured Ford was the most reliable car on the road. But, guess he got a couple of other things the wrong way around too. Sure you want to hear?"

"Go on."

"Well, what they did, him and Bonnie, they swung in a circle, skirting the edges of a couple of states, taking advantage of the state-line rule, you know the one?"

"Bank robbers got rules?"

"Rule being lawmen from one state can't give chase in another. A good lawyer'd get you off in a minute."

"Okay, but how come a Ford?" She was having fun with him now.

"Well, Clyde loved his Ford V8. Even wrote and told old Henry Ford so. Said, what a dandy car you make, Henry. Told him he drove Fords anytime he could get away with one. Faster and free of trouble. Ford's got all the rest skinned."

"He really tell him that?"

"Yeah, he did. Although, you ask me, there's nothing wrong with a good Buick."

"So, you study the law, and find out how to break it."

"Figures you'd see it that way, smarty pants." Bennie turned on his side, looking at her. "See, it was mostly sharp thinking on Clyde's part, except in the end he put trust in the wrong fella, and maybe didn't know when to quit. And the cops got to this wrong fellow and set up that ambush."

"Could have stepped out with their badges and guns and made them stop and give up. Send them to prison."

"Not how the FBI and the Texas Rangers like to think. Strikes a nerve with that J. Edgar Hoover as soon as you cross a state line. And that man doesn't like the hero image some bank robbers get — taking from the rich, giving to the poor. Why he likes to paint them as public enemies."

"That what you want to be, a public enemy?"

"Like I said, if you don't want to do it, we don't need to talk on it."

"Well, maybe I need to think on it. Now you gonna just keep on talking or what?"

nine

AUGUST 16, 1938

Wedded at the Pipestone courthouse across the Minnesota border, August 3rd, it started as the best day of her life. Putting it off, she finally made the telephone to call to Topeka, Stella drew a breath and told her mother she was hitched now. Hattie sounded like she was in need of salts, asked if Stella took a knock to the head, reminding her it didn't count on account she was underage at the time. Stella saying she'd be sixteen in a few days — in case her mother forgot her birthday — Stella writing the wrong date of birth on the certificate, said she did it to show how much Bennie meant to her, her commitment to him, saying dates were nothing but numbers.

Letting her mother think she was out on the coast when she was just six hours north of Topeka. Bennie had told her not to call her mother in case the cops had wiretapped Hattie's phone. But Stella kept on about it until finally he said okay, telling her to listen for clicking sounds and be careful what she said about their whereabouts.

The good times didn't last long. He'd been quiet and dark since getting that awful letter same day as the wedding, letting him know his brother Spencer had died suddenly back in April, something about a bowel blockage. Long past the funeral, Bennie drove them east as fast as he could, sombre most of the seventeen hundred miles. Telling her he needed to spend time with the family right then. Stella not saying how she was his family now, or that he was driving back to where he was a wanted man. Stella hoping the cops forgot the name of Bennie Dickson by now. All he'd done was punch some guy at the license office. From the sound of it, that guy had it coming anyway.

Bennie drove to the family cabin on the west side of Lake Benton, inside the Minnesota border, a three-room place, not much more than a shack that looked to be listing to the right. And though it felt crowded in the tiny place, Stella liked the way the family took her in, better than anybody had treated her that last year in Topeka. And they spent some peaceful days with his older brother Darwin, his wife, Frances, and son, James. And along with Spencer's widow, Lillie, and her new baby she'd named Spencer. Stella holding the baby every chance she got, said she wanted to get the feel for it. Pretending to bite baby Spencer's fingers, then kissing those tiny digits, making smooching sounds, getting the baby to belly laugh.

Bennie's mood brightened, being around the family was a tonic for him. Taking her to some woods a few miles from the place, they sat under a tree and talked about having kids of their own once they settled down. Talked about whether they wanted boys or girls, deciding on one of each.

Then he taught her to shoot the .38. Lining tins along an old fence rail on the edge of a field, showing her how to reload and work the safety. Taught her about aim and trigger pull. Stella was quick getting the hang of it and ended up hitting as many tins as he did. Bennie getting back his smile, saying she was a natural. "Anything at all you can't do, lady?"

"Something comes along, I'll let you know." She smiled at him, thinking a moment, then saying, "Matter of fact, I bet I can hit more'n you."

"Yeah, think so, huh? Well, how about we make it interesting? Tell you what, I'll give you two paces, cut down the distance and even the odds a bit."

"How about we do it even, but you want to make it interesting, how about we do it naked?"

"Out here?"

"Sure, unless you're 'fraid of a little chill."

"You can't go shooting naked."

"How come?"

"Well, 'cause it's foolishness, for one. For two, suppose somebody sees?"

"Like who?"

"It's just not done, that's all, lady."

Calling him bashful, she started to unbutton her top.

☾

On the Thursday afternoon, he whispered to her that he was going to visit Spencer's grave, wanted to do it alone this time. And he left her with the family, Stella singing and cooing to the baby. And next morning, he was off again to go see about lining up a boxing match, this town called Elkton, about a dozen miles west, just over in South Dakota. Telling her there could be a purse with some decent money. Stella knowing they could use it.

Coming back holding a greasy bag of hamburgers, enough for everybody, saying he picked them up at a stand on his way back, a place called Hetland Hamburgers. Long gone cold. Stella heated them in a pan on the wood stove, put lots of onions on his, while Frances and Lillie whipped together a salad and a jug of lemonade to go with it.

Tugging him aside, Stella said, "Thought we were near out of money, going from poor to broke, and you're going out buying hamburgers?"

"Well, I went to that gym in Elkton like I said, a place of sweat and high hopes, and the guy managing it said he might get me sparring with one of his club fighters, see if I'm any good, maybe put me on a Saturday night card. Said he expects me to pay for training. Told him I already got plenty of that, gone a hundred rounds between Chicago and L.A. with an eight-and-one record. And this two-bit from Elkton just grins and says yeah, but he still never heard of me. So I said, pick any of your boys here, don't matter about the weight class, and put your money where your mouth is. Told him I was set to go right then. So, I stripped my shirt, stepped in against the club favorite, a light heavyweight, Sam somebody. Gave me two-to-one odds, so I bet what I had on me, doubling my money."

"Guess you won, huh?"

"Guy had no style. In spite of his size, I went inside, hit him with my one-two pop and down he went. Easy money." Bennie taking his Life Savers, flipping one from the pack, catching it in his mouth.

Before dusk, he took her out to the car next to the barn, opened the trunk and showed her a shotgun and another pistol.

"Guess we're back to that, huh?" Stella said, guessing where most of the fight money had gone.

"I'm not gonna hide it from you, lady. We agree or we don't, but, let me finish, okay? On the drive out, I see they got this bank called the Corn Exchange, and I stopped for a look-see. Walked in and said I was thinking of doing some business, just didn't say what kind. Then went and sat in the car and counted the folks going in and coming out. Only a couple of employees working behind the cages and no security. Local cop station with just a couple cars out front, and a nice and easy way out of town. I came away with a good feeling."

"All these folks packing up for California, looking for a better life, leaves me wondering who's got money to put in a bank?"

"Well, you'd be wondering wrong. A lot of folks going in and out of the place. Anyway, I can see you still got your doubts." Seeing the worry in her eyes.

"First off, you said you were paying respects, then going to see about some matches, not getting in one. Now you tell me about a bank you want to rob."

"Did go and see Spencer, like I said. And yesterday, I did go see about lining up a fight. Guy rubbed me the wrong way, is all. And the bank just happened to be there. Like I said, I had a look, in case we change our mind about it. One thing's sure, we go in, we don't want to go in the wrong way, no place for making mistakes."

"And this?" Stella looked at the shotgun in the trunk. "It just happen to fall in here?"

"Well, Mrs. Smart Guy." Johnny raised the twin barrels halfway from the trunk. "I figure, we go in with pistols it'll get the job done, but let's say we get chased, this bad boy's just the thing for taking care of moving cars."

"Doesn't exactly answer my question."

"Got it at the hardware. Told the guy I was going to bag some ducks. Got it and a box of shells." Bennie admitted it took most of the cash, calling it an investment in their future, then said, "Oh, and I saw a sign for a traveling show coming through, promising to be a gala event, thought maybe I'd take you. Got enough left for it."

"A traveling show, huh?"

"Happy Mustard's show. They got a strongman, midgets, fortune tellers, the sideshows, the whole bit. Cotton candy, you ever have that?"

Thinking she could get tired of him winking like that, doing it like it was cute, saying to him, "And how about a sack, you get one of those too? You know, for all that bank loot." Stella got a flash of skipping down the street back home, that Roller Mills flour sack in her arms. Sure seemed like a long time ago.

. . . *ten*

AUGUST 25, 1938

Three weeks since they walked up the courthouse steps, Bennie driving the dusty stolen Ford past the dead cornfields, coming to a crossroads, turning off the dusty two-lane and pulling into Elkton. The town only about a square mile, the north-south streets all bearing animal names, the main drag called Elk, Bennie passing Badger and Antelope, stopping a half a block from the Corn Exchange bank. Had studied a map of the back roads and figured an easy getaway for his V8. Checking the silver watch he took from the Peerless Laundry back in Los Angeles, Bennie tucked it in the bib pocket of his overalls, looking out the windshield, taking a final look around. Then got out.

Stepping out, Stella straightened the straw hat and dark glasses, Bennie wanting them to look like drifters, something to throw off the cops. Stella not thinking much of the look, taking the newspaper-wrapped package like he told her, and she went along the opposite sidewalk, acted like she didn't know him, just a gal doing some shopping. Her hands shaking so much she thought she'd drop the package.

Not looking over as he rumbled by her, seeing the California plate he'd muddied up, guessed he thought of everything. Clear on what she had to do, seeing Bennie turn around in the street and pull up out front of the Corn Exchange.

"Here we go." Stepping past a group of girls, she considered they might be laughing at her, dressed in overalls with the dumb straw hat and dark glasses. Feigning interest in garden tools in the Elkton Hardware's picture window, she caught the reflection of the bank's front in the glass. Watched him getting out of the car and walking into the Corn Exchange, doing it with purpose, not giving a look around now. She considered he was more Johnny than Bennie right then.

Swallowing back the angst she felt, remembering what he told her, how no wife of his was spending her birthday dirt poor. Said once they got clean away, he'd take her on a shopping spree she wouldn't believe, let her pick out something nice ahead of her birthday tomorrow. "Can't do it up right if we got no money, can we?"

Hard to argue that.

Bennie's first idea was to drive to the next town, Brookings, and book a room and stay the night. Tomorrow being her birthday, he didn't intend to spend it packed in that tiny cabin with all his family. Wanted to do her birthday right and take her to the fanciest place around for supper.

She'd pushed away thoughts of county jail bars, mugshots and fingerprints, Stella pictured the two of them eating ice cream and cake tomorrow night. Guessing only a minute had passed since he'd gone in the bank, she crossed the street and stood by the Ford, the engine still running. Doing like

Bennie told her, she kept watch, giving a slow glance one way, then the other, making like she was waiting on somebody, acting like she didn't have a care, the .38 inside the wrapped newspaper.

Supposed to whistle if she saw anybody going to the door. And when Johnny came running out, she was to jump in the passenger side, and they'd roar off, simple as that. The biggest thing to happen in Elkton since founding day, the townsfolk not knowing what to do. By the time the law strapped on their holsters, she and Bennie would have stirred dust along twenty miles of back road. Mapping the escape route out ahead of time, he had it in his head, telling her it was easy as pie, told her to start thinking what she'd like for her birthday. Anything at all. Stella trying to picture herself in a new outfit, something that wasn't overalls and a straw hat. Forcing herself to think of getting her hair done in a bob with the finger waves, maybe a pair of peep-toe shoes, or her own red lipstick. Remembered her mother saying how a woman had to be a good steward of her husband's money.

☾

"Here we go," saying it to himself. Should be tense, but now that he was walking in the place, he was feeling cool about it. Maybe it was having her along that boosted his conviction. His shoes clanked on the wood floor. Looking around, nobody in the office behind the ribbed glass, just a female customer at the wicket, cashing a check. Just one bank employee in sight, the man on the other side of the wicket, helping the customer. Bennie was pretty sure the place had no alarm, no security man either. Walking to teller window one, he waited behind the woman in a flower dress, her gray hair in a tight bun.

The cashier was thanking her for her patronage, calling her Mrs. Hurd. She hadn't noticed Bennie behind her, or wasn't bothered that he was waiting. Calling the bank employee Robert, she asked how his wife was faring. He told her she was much better now, his eyes shifting behind her, seeing Bennie waiting, smiling to him. Mrs. Hurd went on about having them over for tea sometime.

The brass plate on the counter said the man was Robert Petschow. Mid-thirties, nicely dressed and acting professional. Telling Mrs. Hurd he'd be sure to speak to his better half that very evening and make the arrangements, handing her the twenty dollars, counting it out slow.

Re-counting the bills, Mrs. Hurd talked of a dandy recipe for peach cobbler, Robert glancing at Bennie and smiling again.

This was it, or he'd lose his nerve. Bennie drew the big Colt, his wedding ring clicking the stock. He let the old woman see it, her eyes bugging at the black hole that decided life or death. Stepping to the second wicket, Bennie poked the barrel through, saying to Robert, "Hate to interrupt you, my good man, but I'm sure to have a busy day ahead."

Mrs. Hurd cupped the hand with the bills to her mouth, letting out a moan, and looking like she was about to pass out.

"That peach cobbler you're talking about, ma'am," Bennie said to her. "What flour you use?"

It took a moment, then she said, "Why, Old Glory, only kind I use."

Bennie nodded and said, "Yeah, guess that's a good one, but you ought to try Rollers Mill." Pulling the sewn-together sacks from a pocket. "You make dresses from yours?"

"Know some who have," she said, gulping. "Sewed an apron from one a while ago."

"Amazing the things you can do with them, huh?"

Holding out her twenty dollars in a shaking hand, wanting to drop it in his sack.

"No, ma'am. You worked hard for it. You go on and keep it. Going to need it to bake your pies."

"You're not robbing us?" Robert Petschow said, looking confused, but relieved, his hands half in the air.

"Not you folks, just the bank. Now, how much you got in the drawers, Robert?"

Getting past being bewildered, Robert said, "Well, about fourteen hundred this time of day."

Bennie pushed the sack at him, saying, "Well, I'll just make a withdrawal then."

Interrupted by the front door opening, Bennie half-turned with the pistol, wondering what in the world Stella was doing out there, supposed to give a whistle, let him know when someone was coming in behind him. It was a teenage boy, not much younger than Stella. Froze when he saw the pistol.

Waving the barrel, Bennie told him, "Be a good fellow and stand next to Mrs. Hurd here, would you?"

The boy nodded, eyes affixed to the hole at the end of the barrel, a look of being thrilled scared.

Vaulting over the counter, making it showy, Bennie told Robert Petschow to get a move on. Watching him get to work, clearing out the two tellers' drawers. Taking a look around, Bennie spotted the big gray vault against the back wall. "How about that?"

"The vault?"

"Yeah, I know what it is. And I bet she's full of money."

"Well, sure it is, it's just that—"

"How about you skip giving me the business, and get her

opened up." Bennie thinking he should've had Stella sew up another sack.

"Can't do it."

"How you mean can't?"

"It's on a time lock, sir." Robert Petschow moved his hand slow and checked his watch, saying, "Opens on its own, only it won't be for nearly a half hour."

"The hell's a time lock?"

"It's supposed to keep us from, uh, getting robbed."

"And you expect me to just wait around?"

"Guess the idea's that you won't." Robert added, "Was never in favor of the lock myself."

Reaching in the bib of his overalls, Bennie took his own watch in his free hand, sighing. "Guess we'll just wait then."

"Well, you can't just wait."

"Why, there a rule about it?"

"No, I mean, you hang around, and you'll get caught for sure."

"How about you just keep on filling the sack." Bennie watched him open and empty the second drawer. Saying, "Was a woman working in here the other day."

"Yuh, that'd be Elaine." Robert turned to the desk behind him, an open ledger on top. Saying, "I sent her on errands, just ahead of you coming in."

"You got an alarm hidden someplace? And best be truthful now."

"No, sir. Not sure why we don't. Bank got robbed seven years back, but the president never bothered installing an alarm, just the time lock, said something about lightning not striking the same spot." Stopped talking when the door opened, saying, "Ah, that's Elaine now." Asking if he should go explain the situation to her, didn't want her fainting on the floor. Handing the filled sack to Bennie.

"Yeah, that'd be fine. Just nothing dumb, okay?" Bennie set the sack on the counter, wondered what Stella was doing out there.

Robert went and told Elaine Lovesy, said it would be alright, asked her to go stand behind the second wicket and just act natural. Then he got behind the first one, saying to Bennie, "This be alright? Make it look natural, in case somebody else comes in."

"Yeah, that's a fine idea, Robert. You're one smart fellow. And anybody else comes in, how about you tell them I'm a . . ."

"Bank inspector," Elaine said.

"Yeah, that'd work. Tell 'em that." Holding the pistol out of sight below the counter, Bennie had another look at his watch, the minutes crawling too slow. Bennie looking up as the door opened again.

The look of a farm hand, dusty boots and coveralls, the man walked in and took out some bills, wanting to make a deposit. Coming to Robert's wicket, nodding hello to Mrs. Hurd and the teenage boy standing to the side.

Calling him Teddy, Robert told him his banking would have to wait, right now he was with the bank inspector.

"There's two of you, ain't there?" Meaning him and Elaine.

Teddy caught a glimpse of the pistol behind the counter, Bennie lifting it and pointing it at him, saying, "Actually, I'm making a sizable withdrawal, Teddy, and hope you don't mind the wait."

It took him a moment, but Teddy lifted his rough hands, holding the money for Bennie to take.

"He won't be taking your money, Teddy," Robert said. Then looked to Bennie, realizing he had overstepped. "I get that right?"

"That's right." Bennie told Teddy to step over to the side of the lobby and get on the floor where he could see him. With his arms up, Teddy stepped past another woman coming in, the woman giving him an odd look. Elaine saying to Bennie it was her sister Shirley. Bennie letting Elaine go and explain to her sister she wouldn't be taking her usual break on account of the holdup, advising her sister to get on the floor next to Teddy, told them they could look at each other, but no talking.

Checking his watch again, Bennie shook it like maybe it stopped. The longest half hour of his life.

Next man through the door walked with a limp. Robert saying to Bennie this was TJ, owner of the TJ Pool Hall, telling the man he was sorry for the inconvenience, but asked him to get comfortable on the floor next to Shirley there.

"How you want me to do that with a bum leg?"

Showing the pistol, Bennie said, "Just do the best you can, TJ, and I appreciate you not talking."

Shirley lent a hand, easing TJ down on the floor, Bennie looking at his timepiece again, guessed he should have had Stella Mae demonstrate her whistle before he stood her sentry by the door. Just had it in his mind she'd be able to do it, with the two fingers like you do when hailing the peanut guy's attention at the ballpark. Guessing she'd never been to a ballgame.

The door opened again, and she was coming in, carrying the newspaper package, the .38 starting to poke out.

Coming around the counter, Bennie tugged her aside and told her to act like he didn't know her. In a low voice, saying, "You forget how to whistle?"

"Mouth's so dry, I couldn't get it to work. Hey, it's my first time, okay? All these people coming in, and you not coming out. Thought maybe you need me."

Bennie told her about the time lock.

"The hell's that?"

"Tell you after it pops."

"Looks like we got plenty in the sack." Seeing the flour sack on the counter. Stella looking to the door, eager to get out of there, not wanting to hold the package, the pistol getting heavy.

"Just a few more minutes." Bennie took her by the arm, raising his voice, saying, "You just get on over there, miss, and stand by the door." Then whispering, "How about lick your lips and work on that whistle?"

Standing by the door, she watched the Ford through the glass, gray puffs coming from its exhaust, looked like it was shuddering, idling all this time. Tried to whistle when a couple of men walked to the door, waving her arm, getting Bennie's attention.

Stepping across the floor, heels clicking loud, Bennie acting like he was greeting them, showing the butt of the revolver tucked behind his bib, "See what I got here, boys? You put the rest together, okay?" He pointed over to the lobby floor, waiting till the two went and lay at the end of the row.

"Three more," Stella called, smiling as more men entered through the door, looking at the people lined on the floor. One of them asking what the hell was going on.

Robert Petschow came around, helping out, saying, "Hello gents, come on in. Afraid there's a bit of a holdup."

"What kind of holdup?" the bald one said, unhappy about the delay.

"This kind," Bennie stepped across the lobby, showing the pistol.

"I just came for my money," the younger of the three said, going slack-jawed at the sight of the pistol, holding two checks and a deposit book.

"Came for the same thing." Bennie asked the man's name, taking the checks and deposit book, looking at its balance. "Well, Roy Kramer, no offense, but it don't look like you can stand being robbed."

"No, sir. I guess not."

Putting the checks in the book and handing it back, Bennie told Roy to get on the floor with the others. Then asking the bald man to turn out his pockets. The man was Dunn, the postmaster and druggist. Bennie asking Petschow to show him the bank's ledger, the three of them stepping to the table, looking at the open ledger, confirming Dunn had but twenty bucks in his account, plus the ten in his hand.

"That all you got?" Bennie asked.

"Well, sir, times are hard, but I guess you know it," Dunn said.

"Guess I do." Letting him keep his money, Bennie stepped to the last man, Maurice Campbell saying he managed the city liquor store.

"City, huh? Business any good?" Bennie took a deposit pouch from him.

"Guess it's alright. I just run the place for the county. People come and drink and forget, you know how it is."

"Not much of a drinking man myself." Bennie looked inside the pouch, slipped it in his overall pocket, deciding it belonged to the city. Told the men to go and grab a piece of floor, watching them do it.

Looking out the front, Stella tried to whistle, gave a cough this time, got Bennie looking as a well-dressed man entered. Robert Petschow coming from behind the cashier's counter again, introduced bank president Lester Foreman.

"What in Sam Hill ..." Lester stopped and assessed things, then tried to turn and run.

Blocking him with the package, the pistol barrel sticking out, Stella said, "Want to guess what I got here, mister?"

Coming behind him, Bennie said, "A couple minutes and your time lock'll pop, and we'll be out of your hair."

"I'll see you in prison, or worse."

"Why, you a crook too?" Stella said.

Bennie shoved the Colt at him, told Lester there wasn't much worse than prison, then told him to get on the floor, deciding he didn't like the man much.

"Not going do it, not in this suit," Lester said, crossing his arms.

Pressing the barrel into his stomach, Bennie leaned close and said, "Sure is a nice suit, Mr. Foreman. And it's gonna be a shame to blow a hole in it, mess it all up on you." Pulling back the hammer, Bennie watched Lester Foreman acting indignant for a couple more seconds, his cheeks going red. Then he turned and went to the lobby and pulled the knees of his trousers and got stiffly on the floor, Shirley helping him.

A couple more customers came in, Robert Petschow getting them settled on the floor, didn't want to see anyone getting shot, asking everybody to just stay down and calm. "It'll be over in a few more minutes." A dozen men and the boy in a row on the floor, Bennie allowing Shirley to sit in one of the chairs along the wall, offering Mrs. Hurd the other one. Soon as the watch hand marked the time, he hurried Robert Petschow to the vault, finding it hadn't sprung. Bennie checking his watch again, breathing to ease the rising panic when he heard the lock pop.

"Thank God," the two men said at the same time. And Bennie yanked the vault door, telling Petschow, "You keep an eye. Anyone makes a move, I'm gonna shoot you first, you believe it?"

"Yeah, I believe it."

Ducking into the vault, he stuffed the cotton sack, keeping an eye on Petschow. Going back out and setting the stuffed sack on the counter, he told Stella to stay by the door, then he herded everybody from the lobby and into the vault, making Lester Foreman wait for the three women to go ahead, saying, "Didn't your mother teach you nothing, tubby?"

Elaine giggled and wished him luck.

Lining the hostages down an inner staircase to a lower compartment, Bennie crammed them in, apologized for their troubles and inconvenience, then closed the vault door. And Bennie and Stella walked out easy, Bennie pushing the sack behind the passenger seat, saying, "You did fine, lady, just fine. A real natural at it." Getting in and restarting the stalled Ford, he leaned across the seat and kissed her, asking how she was doing.

"Bet it took ten pounds off. Armpits are sweating fierce."

Bennie saying he'd personally draw her a bath, Stella said she'd rather count what they had in the sack, more money than she'd ever seen in her life. Lots of time for bathing later.

Hanging his arm out the window, Bennie breezed them out of town, saying, "Got a place we can lie low a few days."

"Uh, you forgetting something?"

"Forgetting what?"

"My birthday, you promised me a present."

"Thought you were kidding."

"Nothing funny about not keeping your word."

"Expect me to just pull over and start shopping?"

"Wouldn't shop in this two-bit town, but you said something about Brookings and maybe spending the night in a nice place. Guessing they got shops there. And hey, how about closing your window, I'm getting hair in my mouth?"

"How about, try closing your mouth." He grinned at her.

Opening the trunk, Bennie dropped the pistols into the top of the sack. Reaching a banded stack of bills, he shoved it in a pocket. Slinging the sack over his shoulder, he figured it lent the look of a couple going to do their laundry, her hooking his opposite arm, the two of them walking along the sidewalk, both in overalls, taking a casual look around Brookings, twenty miles east of Elkton.

Busy streets of cars and people going by didn't allow him a chance to count it, Bennie remembered Robert Petschow saying something about fourteen hundred. Walking Stella across to the Dodger Fry House with its big picture window. Looked like a fitting place for a birthday supper, asking the waitress about some place to get their laundry done after.

Sitting against the back wall, he shoved the sack onto the seat next to him and spooned up his chowder, hardly tasting it, looking past the tables, one eye on the front door, the other out the window, the Ford right across the street. Stella having a salad, going on about what they just did, and how her mother would have a fit if she could have seen it. Bennie ordering them both sirloin, medium rare, with a baked potato.

"Sure works up an appetite, huh? I'm starved." Then saying Stella could go for the custard after. "No need to mind your figure. Not today."

"What's that mean?"

"Anybody deserves it, I guess it's you." Smiling, Bennie was thinking about switching cars, wanting to drive east, rethinking about staying in Brookings, betting the law would widen its search, looking for a couple in a black Ford.

"Just the best birthday I ever had," she said, slicing into her steak, calling the waitress, saying they could do with more biscuits, asking about the custard. Then to him, "Life's just about perfect."

"How you mean just about?"

"Well, one day we're walking in the courthouse and tying the knot, then going in the bank and coming out rich. And all ahead of me turning sixteen. How many girls can say a thing like that? And this meat, it sure is good, ain't it?"

"Yeah, you bet it is."

"Just one thing . . ."

The fork stopped on the way to his mouth.

"This present, the one you talked about. Just wondering what you were thinking?" Calling him Johnny.

"Johnny when you want a present, huh?" Smiling, this girl thinking about shopping for her birthday, with a manhunt going on.

"More like Bennie when you're bad, and Johnny when you're good. Sometimes I think it's the other way around."

"Yeah, so which one you like best?"

"Depends, I guess."

"Well, you just go find a fitting shop and pick out something nice."

"Was a place on the way in, sign said sundry, guess it's got women's apparel."

Thinking of a different kind of peril, but going along, keeping his word, he said that sounded fine.

"Sure could stand to get out of these." Meaning the overalls. "And maybe they got a nice pair of shoes to go along. That too much?" She looked for a reaction, not getting one, then saying, "And this hat's got the look like a goat nipped at it."

Bennie figured she earned the whole ensemble, saying, "Can't have my wife going around looking Okie. You just finish your custard, and you go and find yourself something nice, the whole shebang."

"Almost sounds like I'm going on my own."

"Got to take care of a thing. You just go on, I'll catch up." Pushing away his plate, smiling at her, his foot tapping against the table post. He was picturing the looks of Whitey Kyle and the men he knew at the Missouri State Pen, imagined what they'd think about being twenty miles from the bank he just robbed, having a sit-down lunch and talking about going shopping. Looking out the window, he looked at a man in a suit walking by, something about the way the man was looking around, Bennie guessing they ought to be fifty miles from here and racing for more. Had mapped the back roads in his mind, thinking they could hide out at the family farm, the property on his mother's side, about seven miles from the cabin at Lake Benton. They ought to be fine there for a couple of days.

"You not gonna eat that?" Looking at the piece of meat on his plate.

"Slows my thinking when my stomach's doing all the grinding."

"Can't say what's got in me, don't usually pack it down like this. I guess this line of work brings it out."

"Line of work, huh?"

Sliding her empty plate aside, she took his. "Although it's likely to cause trouble getting the dress size right."

Bennie grinned, thinking it had to be why he loved her — the girl being natural, along with good looking. Liked her edge, and she was smart and funny too. Paying the bill and leaving a fat tip from the holdup money, he hefted the sack and took her arm, asking the waitress which way to the sundry.

"Thought you said laundry?" the girl said, thanking him for the tip.

"Laundry for me, sundry for my wife."

The girl giving them directions.

Out the door, he slipped Stella some bills and said he'd meet up. Stella holding back her questions, just had to trust in him.

Going the opposite way down the block, he gripped the sack and put it up on his shoulder and walked past the Ford, not giving it the time of day. He'd seen the man in the suit as soon as he stepped from the Dodger Fry House, pulled the hat low to block the late sun, glad Stella just walked the other way, not asking questions.

The man stopped along a low wall, other side of the street. Wasn't there when Bennie parked the Ford. Leaning against the bricks half a block up, the man cupped his hands to light a smoke, looked like he was trying to fit in. Lawman written all over him, that bulge under the open suit jacket. Crossing the street, Bennie trudged closer to him, putting a limp into his step.

Moving along the line of parked cars, noting the bank up the block, looking about twice the size of the one in Elkton, folks coming and going like ants. Stopping next to the man, Bennie rested the sack on the ground, puffing air like he was tired, asking, "Don't mean to trouble you, mister, but you know of a laundry hereabouts? Wife says it's here someplace."

"A what?" The man smiled and took him in, puffing on his smoke.

"Laundry mat, you know? Wife told me I got to pitch in. Guess you know the drill."

"Sure, I do." The man shook his head, grinned, and said, "Appeasing the missus, that's a job alright."

"Can say that again. Hey, you think I could bum one of those?"

The man said sure, put his smoke between his lips, took his pack of ready-rolls and offered the Chesterfields to Bennie.

"Says she's got her hands full with the kids. Between you and me, guess I don't see the fuss, my old mother had six of us, and no laundry mats back in those days." Tapping the pack, putting one in his mouth, handing it back, saying, "Thanks, pal. Yeah, had just an old scruff board back then, you know what I mean?"

"Yeah, remember them, and I hear what you're saying."

The two of them blowing smoke.

"Johnny O'Malley," Bennie said, sticking out his hand.

"Werner Hanni," the man said back, shaking the hand.

"I guess a couple years of the ball and chain, and a man learns not to argue," Bennie said. "And here I go, walking around with the laundry, for all I know a load of her dainties." Looking up the street. "Sure she said it was on this block, maybe the next one. Guess I got to pay more attention when she talks, what she keeps telling me."

"Well, I wish I could help you, chum," Werner said. "But being married on my double go-round, guess I'm the wrong one to ask. And I can't help you with the laundry either. Not from around here actually, just visiting. But you might go in that bake shop and ask."

Bennie looked over, saw some heads behind the glass, saying it was a good idea, wishing Werner a good day, took a final drag, dropped the butt under a shoe, hefted his sack and hobbled across the street toward the shop, remembering his limp. When he came out, he gave Werner Hanni a wave and kept on walking, adjusting the sack on his shoulder again, remembering to add the limp. Keeping an eye out, sure Werner Hanni's kind of lawman traveled in packs. When he was safely up the block and out of view, Bennie was back to looking at the cars parked along the curb. Trying to guess which one had a V8.

(

"Well, look at you," he said, walking into Maisel's Sundry and down its center aisle.

"Thought you gave up on me after seeing me eat like that," Stella said, pecking him on the cheek, standing before the long mirror in high-waisted slacks, a white silk blouse, white T-strap shoes and a tan beret tilted on her head, saying it was more everyday than a dress. "Don't you think?" Acting like she hadn't just robbed the Elkton bank, then asking what happened to his laundry.

"Put it in the car."

Stella wondering why he didn't leave it in there in the first place, the pretty salesgirl ringing up the sale, folding the old clothes into a bag. Stella put down the bills he gave her, Bennie reaching in his pocket for the roll, making up the difference, and took the shopping bag and led Stella out, glancing around before stopping at a green Buick at the corner and opening the passenger door. No sign of Werner Hanni or his kind.

"What about the Ford?"

"Traded it in. Buick's a little more everyday than the Ford, don't you think?" Going and slipping behind the wheel, the ignition wires hanging from under the steering column.

... *eleven*

AUGUST 26, 1938

"She was taller than me." Betty Walsh showed how much with her hand, listening to the man's question, saying, "The car, oh, I don't know, mister . . . guess it was dark, maybe black and dirty-looking. No, I can't say what kind. I'm twelve, you know." She squinted one-eyed up at the man in the suit and serious hat. He called himself Werner Hanni, had showed her his badge and said he was with the FBI, asking his questions.

Looking up at his tie falling from his suit jacket, flapping like it was trying to touch her, Betty said, "One thing, she walked with her hips funny, you know, going side to side, the way some girls do. Just thought she looked like she was putting it on, how my momma would call it.

"Well, overalls, the kind a man wears, you know, and a straw hat like a hitchhiker. Uh huh, dark glasses so I couldn't see her eyes. Said to her as she passed by, never seen you around before, and she says back, that's right, you never seen me. Walked right by me and crossed the street, went over there. Thought she was being kind of highbrow.

"License plate, oh, I don't know, mister. People notice things like that, license plates?" Betty reminding him of her age, then asked if it was alright to go home now, looking at his flapping tie again. Seeing the state trooper coming from the bank, walking up behind the FBI man. Betty guessing here came some more questions, getting tired of talking about it.

"The package, guess it was about like so, wrapped up, newspaper, thought maybe it was a present. Mother does it that way, with the day-old dailies, when we got no wrap. That's all I know, mister. You want to, you ought to go ask Jean or Connie. Were standing right there with me, saw her same as me."

Werner Hanni thanked the girl and looked at the approaching trooper, the hat with the badge on it, utility belt over the uniform jacket, the stripes on the sleeve.

Held out his big hand and told Hanni he was Sergeant Picton, then saying, "You got what you need, agent, we can take it from here." Giving the local lawman's tolerant smile.

"Well, I got all the confidence that you can, Sergeant, but I'm afraid this one's going federal, and I mean nothing personal by it, but the only thing you're taking's a walk. No offense."

"No offense, huh?" Smiling now like he was being patient, Dale Picton looked down at Betty, called her by name, told her she could run along, then looked back at Werner Hanni, not so friendly now, saying, "That's how the chief'll want to play it."

"Your chief, huh? Well, I got a call from the attorney general's office right after it happened, fellow's name's William

Gordon, maybe you heard the name. Doesn't matter, anyway, that man's not playing, calling the holdup a violation of the National Bank Robbery Act. Told me to get my butt down here, write a report and get back to him pronto. Said his next call's to J. Edgar, and between you and me, that man's a bigger chief than yours any day of the week, right up there with . . ." Werner glancing heavenward, saying, "Guess you get what I'm saying." Then he eased up. "Look, Sarge, the whole mess's got to do with the Federal Deposit Insurance Corporation insuring the Corn Exchange, something like that, making it federal or whatever you locals want to call it. The bottom line's I got sent down here and I'm expected to report back. And that's what I'm doing. You want more, then I guess we best go see your chief. Just give me a minute while I call the attorney general back, let him know we got a snag."

"Heck, you people and your snags. We put out an all-points and a patrol'd run them two to ground in no time, have them cuffed and hand them to you on a plate. How's that for solving your snag?"

"Yeah, unless it turns out like that time you locals took it on yourselves and went after Dillinger, that bank in Sioux Falls, you remember it? Well, was him and Baby Face driving through town with hostages on the running boards, waving at folks like it was a parade float. Made off with just shy of fifty grand. Guess the locals got caught napping on that one." Werner Hanni shrugged like it could happen to anybody. "Was federal agents that gave chase and put an end to it."

"Yeah, know the kind of end it was too. Dillinger got gunned down, armed with a ticket stub. And Nelson got it pretty much the same way. You federal boys don't take chances, I guess. And so you know, I was chummy with one of the men wounded in, what you call, that napping in Sioux Falls, so maybe you want to watch what you say."

"Yeah, I guess we all got stories. Could tell you about Ed Hollis, agent I knew, in on stopping Nelson, one of three killed bringing that man to ground. Look, maybe we got started the wrong way, Sergeant," Hanni said. "I guess we got the same job to do. Just saying, the bureau's putting its full attention on this one. And what I hear from Gordon, this one came from the top. J. Edgar's not keen on bank robbers running around and coming off looking like Robin Hood. Burns the man's butt hairs."

"Yeah, I guess I heard that, and you don't mind me saying so, there could be something wrong with that man, your chief," Picton said. "Just based on what I heard."

"Well, guess you're free to say it, Sergeant, but me, I can't even think it." Werner Hanni hesitated, then offered his hand again.

Picton looked at it, then shook it, saying, "Guess you're right, we're all on the same side," then turned and walked to his patrol car.

. . . *twelve*

AUGUST 27, 1938

"A m I talking plain enough for you, Hamm, or you need me to slow down?"

"It's Hanni, sir. And no, I'm hearing you fine." Wishing he hadn't come in early on a Saturday, his one day off, and dumb enough to pick up the phone. Werner Hanni looked around the empty outer office, most of the lights off. Same way he'd picked up that call a week ago, William Gordon from the attorney general's office. This was the second call from the director in a week, wanting an update, didn't matter it wasn't his case.

Werner Hanni was starting to understand why the higher-ups called Hoover "Speed" behind his back, the man talking a hundred miles a minute. According to the office chatter, there were a couple long-timers like Appel who dared call him "Speed" to his face, the rest doing it behind his back. Another rumor was the nickname stuck from Hoover's younger days, when he delivered groceries as a kid. Not employed by the grocery, young Edgar stood holding the door and helping the elderly carry sacks of groceries to their cars, wagons or right to their homes, earning his tips. One of Hanni's trainees suggested "Speed" spoke fast to mask a stutter. Somebody more charitable saying the nickname came from Hoover's high school days, for his dexterity on the football field.

"This man Gordon at the attorney general's wants to know our progress, calling me direct," Hoover said. "A man like that addressing a man like me, talks like he's taking notes. Asked how the fugitives slipped through, talking like one bank robbery's a crimewave. Forgetting who stopped the Barkers and Dillinger and that Baby Face, put a stop to all those sons of bitches. Was right there when we took down Karpis, you saw it."

"Was right there, yes, sir." Werner Hanni having the misfortune of being among the ten agents that took Alvin "Creepy" Karpis that day, first of May, two years ago. The agents armed to the teeth, but not one bringing handcuffs. Hanni guessing nobody expected Karpis to walk out of there and just give up. The director had flown in for the attempted arrest, his men told to stake out the Karpis hideout, not make a move till he arrived. Treating it like a publicity stunt, ducking behind one of the FBI cars across the street, along with a newsman with his press camera. Hoover waited till Karpis came out and got in his car, was swarmed by the ten agents. Then dashing across the street, Hoover called out, "I'll take it from here, boys." And made the arrest. The flashbulb popped, catching the director's double row of smiling teeth, showing in the evening news under the headline "Fearless Lawman." When Hoover asked for handcuffs — the newsman popped the dead bulb, pushing in a fresh one — the field agents patted their pockets for cuffs, Werner Hanni dumb enough to pull off his necktie, handing it to the director, suggesting a Windsor knot, just as the bulb popped again. The newsman liked the joke, jotting it down. It appearing like a caption under the shot in the morning edition.

"And what do you suppose I said to this Gordon?" Hoover said over the phone.

"Well, sir, I could—"

"Told him we're tightening the noose, that's what. And I don't mean a Windsor knot. Told him we're working our leads and doing our police work. Told him my agents are out there day and night and closing in. Any idea how that makes me feel, Hamm, having to shovel shit before a man like that?"

"Well, I can only imag—"

"Can you, Hamm? Can you really? How about you imagine where these two-bit bank robbers are hiding. Meantime, I'll just keep my shovel next to my desk. You know, it's got me thinking maybe I got the wrong top man down in Aberdeen."

"Meaning no disrespect, sir, but this case belongs to St. Lou—"

"And we all pitch in, don't we, Hamm? It's what makes the bureau the shining powerhouse of united law enforcement that I made it. Anything less I call pussyfooting. You see it different, Hamm?"

"Guess not, sir."

"If I lift my shoe and see there you are, Hamm, I'm going to take my shovel or find a stick, and I'm going to scrape and flick you off, let you land someplace, some remote outpost. How would that be, Hamm?"

"Wouldn't like it, sir."

"Now, let's see . . ." The sound of a creaking chair over the line. "I'm standing at my wall map, taking a pin and closing my eyes, sticking it in. What d'you know, Juneau, Alaska — you know of it, Hamm?"

"Guess I heard of it, sir." Werner Hanni rolled his eyes.

"Want to bet it gets above zero in June?"

"Wouldn't want to—"

"Well, I see we've got an office there. Never been to it, but I bet it's a couple of desks around a pot-belly. Agents wearing mukluks and hats with the earflaps. Place where the badge freezes in your hand. You like fish, Hamm?"

"I get your point, sir. My office stands ready to—"

"I'm putting you down for mukluks, guessing a size ten. Am I painting a picture, Hamm?"

"You're being perfectly clear, sir."

"Now, let's hear it, your action plan."

Never hearing the term before, Werner Hanni said, "Right after this call, I'll ring SAC Norris in St. Louis, let him know I'm sending a copy of my initial report to Supervisor Metcalfe, ask what my office can do to help."

"And how about you get on the blower and inform all offices in the surrounding states, give them everything we got on the Corn Exchange case. Meantime, I'll keep this transfer note on my desk."

"Yes, sir."

"The man in the White House expects me to crush crime, and he's trusting me to do the job. Can't do it on my own. What I need's the right people."

"Yes, sir."

"Let the crooks know this shit won't stand. They walk in a bank and pull a weapon, they're in for a federal shel-lacking."

"Yes, sir." Werner Hanni pictured the director with his stick and his shovel in front of a dung pile, posing for some newsman's camera.

"And I don't want to read about another Okie bank-robbing hood skipping across state lines and getting the public's sympathy, making fools of my crack agents, getting my phone dancing off the ringer. I want these sons of bitches in a box, you hear me, Hamm?"

"Loud and—"

Werner Hanni heard the line go dead. Slumping back in his swivel chair, he put his fingers to his temples, the ache behind his eyes coming on like the Illinois Central. Thinking he might throw up in his wastebasket.

. . . thirteen

AUGUST 28, 1938

They tore east along the back roads, south past the dry hills and patches of tree lines, east again by drought-dead fields where corn ought to be standing. Raising the dust, crossing into Minnesota, they gassed the stolen Buick up outside of Verdi, at some rickety garage with a Texaco pump. Then he took them north and east again past Lake Benton and the family cabin, skirting the town of Tyler, parking around back of an abandoned cropper's shack he knew. Stella guessing he was being cagey. Screwing up his courage to go see his parents the next day.

After a night of sleeping on car seats, him in front, her in back, they made their way to the Johnson farm, seven miles east of Lake Benton, the place where his mother had grown up. Bennie telling her about life on the farm, the crops and livestock back before the drought. Told her they'd be staying only a few days, long enough for his folks to get to know his girl, maybe get a chance to get in some target practice.

"That what I am, a girl, huh?"

"Well, my girl, but I guess you rob a bank, now you're more woman than girl. Far as the shooting, you got to keep in practice."

"Guess I got a good teacher."

"Taught you a bunch of things."

"That's true, you did." She drew the revolver from under the seat.

Bennie forgetting she even had it under there, the .38 looking big in her hand, but she held it natural enough. Saying, "I got to admit, you're a fair shot."

"Good as you."

"And getting bigheaded too." Raising a brow and clowning with her. Talk helped hide the dread of facing his father, hated thinking he'd disappointed the old man again. His parents grieving over losing one son, now another one wanted by the law again. And he hadn't told them about getting married either.

"The trouble you get me into, it's a good thing to know." Stella slid the pistol back under the seat, recalled that photo she'd seen in the papers: Bonnie Parker pointing that pump gun at Clyde Barrow, reaching for the pistol in his waistband, the two of them hamming for the camera.

"Got to say that's true enough," he said.

"And as I recall, there's a thing or two I taught you."

"Got me there." It had him laughing. Rolling up the county road, Bennie looked up at the house where he grew up, idled his engine down by the mailbox, looking at the place, making sure no lawmen were laying for them. Pulling up the dirt drive, he stopped out front and let Stella out, setting the suitcase on the porch steps, leaving the flour sack in the trunk.

"Okay, so, I'm your girl, but how you going to tell them about this?" Holding up her hand, showing the ring.

"Guess you're gonna see." He pushed her hand back down, trying to not look nervous.

The woman stepping past the screen door was Alma, a handsome woman of solid build, her graying hair tied back in a bun, Stella seeing where Bennie got his looks.

"Well, now look who's come home." Coming off the steps, Alma lit up and took him into her arms, calling through the screen for James to get out here.

"Hey ya, Ma. Aren't you a sight." Bennie grabbed her tight, lifted and swung her in a circle.

Overjoyed seeing her son, Alma wiped tears away from her eyes, play-slapped his arm, noticed Stella and told him to set her down.

Seeing his father come behind the screen door, Bennie went to the steps, holding out his hand. Stiff and formal. James came onto the porch and took his son in a hug, neither saying a word.

"And who've we got here?" His mother held out her hand to Stella, beaming at her.

Bennie saying, "Hold the rail, Ma, this here's Stella Mae, the newest member of the Dicksons." Then introducing his wife to his father.

"Don't tell me . . ." Taken aback, Alma cried some more, then apologizing all over the place.

"Well, I am telling you." Bennie reached over and lifted Stella's hand and showed the ring. "Didn't let this one get away, Ma. And yup, that's a real diamond alright."

Alma was shocked and delighted all at the same time, saying to her husband, "Look at that, will you, James, our boy's got married. Oh my, just let me catch my breath. Well, come on in the house. Let me get a room fixed up, and a pot on. Just in luck, I baked today."

"Could smell it a mile off," Bennie said, winking at his father. Then to Stella, "My ma gets to baking, best step back and look out."

While Alma fussed about the place, James put an arm around his new daughter-in-law and led her into the house, asking how long they'd be staying, wanting to know all about her. Making her feel welcome.

Saying sure to a glass of lemonade, Stella felt herself fitting right in.

After bringing the suitcase in, Bennie went to park the Buick, rolled it behind the barn, out of sight from the county road. Taking the flour sack, he dumped it out in the trunk and counted, shoving a couple bundles in his pockets. Then taking a shovel off a peg, he took the sack and went to find a spot to dig a hole, out past a grove of poplars where the roots weren't too thick, about a hundred yards, out of sight of the house.

Coming back, clapping dirt from his hands, finding Stella sitting on the porch. Pouring him a glass of lemonade from the pitcher on the side table, she asked what he was up to. "I thought maybe you run off." Handed him the glass.

Leaning close, he told her he buried the money, just in case.

"In case of what?"

He just frowned at her.

"My share too?"

"Never thought of it as shares."

"Just thinking I should be in on something like that."

"Right. Okay, how about I sketch you a map, that be alright?"

"Guess you're missing my point." Looking away from him.

Then said he was taking his new wife dancing after supper, the dance held the last Sunday of every month out by Lake Benton, a big red barn all strung with lights, and a local jug band playing.

"You dance, huh?" She brightened.

"Just wait and see." Telling her to wear the new outfit, he said he wanted to show her off to some fellows.

Supper was roast chicken, candied yams, creamed spinach, gravy and biscuits, Bennie borrowing the family truck, leaving the Buick behind the barn. Stopping along a creek, he reached a bag of tin cans from the truck bed, handing her the .38, and setting a half dozen cans on a stump and some rocks, stepping back fifty feet. Shooting the first can with his big Colt, missing the next, sending it spinning with a third shot, then nailing the rest, a single shot each, leaving one standing. "Well, let's see you top that, hot shot."

"Tell me to put on my good outfit, shoes with heels like a handicap, promise me dancing, then take me shooting?"

"You want to take 'em off, go right ahead. You're the one likes doing it naked." He went over to the rail and lined up six more cans.

"Sure can show a gal a swell time, take her shooting when she's thinking about dancing, that's all."

"Plenty time for the two-step. But you need to stay sharp, me too. Now, how about we make it interesting, call it a dime a can?"

"Thought this husband-and-wife thing was about what's mine is yours."

"Yeah, but this is shooting and gambling. What's yours'll be mine soon enough. Now come on, let's see what you got."

Glancing at the cans, she took a two-handed grip and fired, the pistol kicking up. Ringing in her ears. The can was gone. Winking at him, she fired again and knocked away the next one. Then the rest. Then looked at him, saying, "So, how about it, you want to go double or nothing?"

◖

Next day, Bennie was gone in the Buick by the time she got up. He'd left a note on his pillow, writing he was taking care of some business, but didn't say what it was, leaving her at the farm. Stella getting tired of him ducking out, sitting over coffee with Alma, the two of them getting along. Alma never saying anything about the police coming around to look for Bennie, or how he disappeared out to California.

Beating a couple of rugs and sweeping up the plank floors before Bennie came back at noon, with a can of paint and some flowers, a bunch for her, the other for Alma. After a lunch of sandwiches and cake, he set about painting the Buick yellow out behind the barn, stirring the can of paint, telling Stella the cops wouldn't be looking for a yellow car.

"Yellow, huh?" Stella saying the glop smelled as awful as it looked, watched him brush it on.

"What you got against yellow?"

"Kinda stands out, don't you think?"

"Not when they're looking for a green one."

Still light by the time he got cleaned up — using the Red Star Cleaner on his hands, wiping them with a rag, yellow paint still under his fingernails — guessing the paint would dry by morning, not daring to hang around the family home any longer, thinking the cops could come looking. Spent the evening talking about his studies with his father, the two of them discussing books they'd read. His father not asking why anybody would paint a decent car yellow as a banana.

Driving out of Tyler after a late lunch, the yellow paint still sticky, catching dust along the back roads. Six and a half hours before they got to Topeka, the paint looking brown and awful, no shine left on the metal.

On account of the late hour, they took a room in the only place that looked open, a three-story building called the Lucky Inn, Stella saying the only thing lucky was finding a late supper of cheese, bread and stale, hot coffee. Cockroaches scattered when she turned on the room light, and a bedspring was poking through the mattress.

Bennie was back to thinking of lining up some fights, maybe wearing a mask, worried the clubs would paste up posters, showing his likeness, and be a good chance Johnny O'Malley wouldn't get through the first round before the cops came through the ropes with handcuffs. Saying to her, "I guess they still want me for popping that clown at the license office."

"So, what then?" Stella knowing he was leading up to something.

"Well, there is one thing I been thinking about. This bank I saw in Brookings."

She didn't react, just looked at him.

"Well, figure we'd bag enough from it, see us through for a long time."

"You looked it over after robbing the one in Elkton, while I was trying on pants, didn't you?"

"Well, okay, maybe I had a peek while I was hot-wiring the Buick, yeah, couldn't help seeing it. And gave me something to do while you were getting the size right."

Both of them laughing.

... *fourteen*

SEPTEMBER 1, 1938

Werner Hanni sat at his desk with the lamp on, looking out at the lights of Aberdeen, could make out the shape of the dome on the Brown courthouse past the rooftops. Alone in the office again, liked it when the place was quiet, let him focus on his cases, spending the late hours there since the Corn Exchange bank robbery. Feeling triggered by the urgent phone calls from the director. Werner thinking the calls had as much to do with what happened that first day of May, two years ago in New Orleans, right on Canal Street. The capture of Alvin "Creepy" Karpis.

He'd been a trainee then, excited to be in on taking down the most wanted man in America. Staking out the flat for days where Karpis was supposed to be hiding out, the man's Plymouth pulling up to the curb out front.

Ten bureau men held their positions, hiding in an empty store across the street, working shifts between rounds of poker, three men maintaining surveillance from triangulated corners, ordered by the director to contain the situation, not to make the arrest until he showed up to play man in charge. Hoover taking position behind one of the FBI cars across the street when Karpis pulled up, looked like he was picking his teeth, waiting for somebody. The agents swarmed around the Plymouth, pistols and rifles pointing as the fugitive sat behind the wheel.

"I park you boys in?" Karpis said, smiling and planting his hands on the steering wheel.

Stepping from cover, Hoover called, "You're under arrest, you son of a bitch. Go on and flinch, see what happens." Turning to the newsman, saying, "This fish has been hoo—"

The newsman popped his flashbulb, sending the director blinking the rest of the way across the street, his men leveling weapons at the man behind the wheel. The most wanted man in the country. Karpis didn't take his hands from the wheel till Hoover ordered him to do so. Blinded by another flashbulb, Speedy blinked like he had an affliction, addressing Karpis, naming the charges, then he smiled again for the camera, asking for handcuffs as his boys seized Karpis from the car.

Shaking his head, thinking back, Werner Hanni replayed the moment when Hoover asked for the handcuffs, wanting to snap them on as the camera flashed, doing it for the syndicated press. His elite force patting their jacket pockets, not a man had brought handcuffs, none expecting Karpis to give up without a bloody fight. All armed to the teeth, expecting a body bag, not handcuffs. Still not sure why he did it, Werner Hanni unlooped his necktie and held it out to his blinking boss, thinking it was funny, saying, "Here you go, boss, this ought to do the trick. But I were you I'd go for something more than a Windsor knot." Everybody but Hoover laughed, the newsman's flashbulb popped again, Werner Hanni standing in the shot, found himself laughing on the front page.

A couple of years of hard work and he got the promotion to SAC, special agent in charge of the Aberdeen office. Werner guessing the director had forgotten about the Windsor knot crack, busy developing his crime lab, keen on fingerprinting and scouring the shadows for communists. But now, it was all coming back, and Werner was wondering about landing up in Anchorage. In the end, he guessed it was worth it, something he could tell the grandkids if he ever had any. Only thing that didn't sit right was the arrest of Karpis that got Hoover in the public eye in the first place, the press under his thumb deeming him the top cop, and the legend of law enforcement. The director known to pass favors to members of the press who told it his way, the bureau stopping the Kellys and Dillingers and Pretty Boys and Baby Faces, and the Barker family. Had a hand in stopping Bonnie and Clyde too. The media crediting Hoover and his bureau for taking them all down, one crook at a time.

Now, the only game in town, the director was turning his eye on the couple who hit the Elkton bank. And it didn't matter they were a couple of amateurs who got away with just over twenty-one hundred bucks, with nobody getting shot, and the couple not robbing the townsfolk, just the bank.

Hanni guessed what got under Hoover's skin was the public had taken a liking to the couple, same as they did with Bonnie and Clyde — robbing a bank instead of standing in a soup line. From witness statements, it was a handsome man, not too tall with curly hair, mid-twenties, soft spoken and letting folks keep what belonged to them. His accomplice was a pretty blonde in her teens. Hanni thinking of his own daughter, nearing that age and still sleeping with a Raggedy Ann.

. . . *fifteen*

SEPTEMBER 2, 1938

"How you gonna break it to her, about getting hitched?" Bennie asked, taking his eyes from the road and glancing at her, driving to Topeka.

"Already told her, that time I phoned her. Not something you can keep from Mother."

"Uh huh."

She gave him a smile, saying, "Just trying to decide which way to go."

"What way's that?"

"Well, do I say, hey Momma, you remember Johnny O'Malley, or do I call you Bennie Dickson, hope she's gone dim and forgot she already met you as Johnny."

"Guess you think it's funny."

"Then again, with the long line of fellows I brung home all those years, likely won't recall one Johnny from the next. So, wouldn't go worrying about it."

"Well, I'm not worried, but go and rub it in." Bennie smiled, thinking about stealing another car, the yellow paint pocked with dirt and bugs looked like hell, bound to get the wrong kind of attention. Top of that, Bennie was hoping to make a good impression with her folks, smooth things over about the cops coming to their door that time he ditched their daughter and ran off to California.

"Yeah, let's just stick with Bennie," she said.

"You're one funny girl alright."

She held up the wedding band, smiling at him. "Yeah, you went and made a dishonest woman of me." Stella laughed, the car passing the Welcome to Topeka sign, the sun rising in a washed-out sky, not a cloud in Kansas as usual, the empty fields flying past. "Either way, Bennie or Johnny, they get to know you, they're gonna love you same as me."

"Can tell them I'm studying on being a lawyer."

"And it could come in handy, we get caught robbing a bank, you can arrange bail as well as plead our case." Leaning across the seat, she turned his head, giving him a long kiss, kept him from turning his head back to the road, saying, "I got an eye on it, don't worry. What's the matter, you don't trust me?"

"This a new game, huh?"

"Yeah, a game of chance, one I just made up. How you play it, you keep us between the ditches, and let me do the rest." Kissing his ear, not letting him turn his head to see the road, she tugged up his shirt tails.

"Maybe not your best game." Bennie corrected his steering, wheels touching the gravel.

She undid his buttons, pulled out the shirt, kissing his neck, raising herself up and straddling his lap, the steering wheel into her back, honking the horn. "You want me to stop, just got to say so."

Raising his neck to get a look past her shoulder, Bennie with his hands on the wheel, slowing enough and grateful for this empty stretch of two-lane. Nothing but dry ground past the ditches, the car moving at about twenty miles an hour.

At this rate, they wouldn't get to the Redenbaugh place till past dark, not what he should be thinking about right then, but Bennie wanted to get a good look along Clay Street before going to her mother's door, the cops could still be looking. Feeling bad about them coming around her folks' place. Thinking maybe they should get a room at a tourist camp or stay at the old railcar — the one Spencer had dubbed Ben's cabin, a place the two brothers hung out as boys — abandoned in a pasture out by Auburn, just south of Topeka. No running water or electricity, but they'd be safe there. Nobody else knowing about it. Bennie thinking he could bury more money there, after they hit the Brookings bank. Just keep enough to buy a couple of cars, stash them in rented garages in case they needed to make a quick switch. And they could use a couple more aliases. His old man had told him to use his smarts and learn the law, and here he was using it to break it. But he was in it now, and he'd need to throw sand on their trail, not wanting to end like Barrow and Dillinger. Barrow hit fifteen banks, some of them more than once; and Dillinger robbed more than that. Bennie needed a better outcome. Needed to know when to quit.

"Hey, I'm right here," she said, moving against him.

"Like I don't know—" Correcting the steering as the wheels touched the gravel again.

Stella pulling at her own clothes, then slipping him inside, moaning and arching her back and rocking in his lap. Bennie having to stop along the roadside.

☾

Coming to the porch door, Hattie Redenbaugh watched them pull up out front, surprised, then taking in the awful-looking car that looked like it had a five o'clock shadow. Swishing a hand at a moth drawn to the porch light, she touched the hand to her tied-back hair, seeing Stella and her young man step out.

"Hey ya, Momma." Stella getting out, throwing her arms in the air, going to her.

Already in tears, Hattie was calling to Lester inside the house, then coming off the steps, saying, "Why wouldn't you call, let me know . . . oh, never mind that." Running to her and hugging her. "Just don't know who you are anymore."

"Well, seeing you mention it, Mother, I guess I'm Mrs. Bennie Dickson now." Holding out the ring for Hattie to see.

Wiping her eyes with the corner of the apron, Hattie held Stella's hand to the porch light and gawked at it.

Stella reached and hooked hold of Bennie's sleeve, pulling him forward. "You remember Bennie?"

Bennie put out his hand. "Good to see you again, Mrs. Redenbaugh."

"I remember Johnny."

"Yes, ma'am. And there's a story behind it. One I'll be happy to . . ."

"You take a knock to your head, girl?" Hattie was back to looking at Stella. Then, back to him. "You do it, knock her on her head?"

"Oh, Mama, swept me off my feet, is what."

"Lester!" Hattie called into the house, louder this time. "Get yourself here."

It was going better than Bennie expected, hearing Lester trudging down the hall from the kitchen, relieved to see the stepdad wasn't holding a rifle, stepping out onto the porch, taking the steps and hugging Stella. Then he held her at arm's length, gave her a smile and a long look, turned to Bennie, offering his hand, "Johnny, wasn't it?"

"It's Bennie now, sir."

"Well, I thank you for bringing our girl back, Bennie."

"Not all he did." Hattie reached and lifted Stella's hand, showing the ring. Lester raising his eyebrows, surprised and happy.

"I'm Mrs. Bennie Dickson now." Stella smiled at her stepdad, looked like she was enjoying this.

. . . sixteen

SEPTEMBER 11, 1938

"Well, let's see what you got, baby." Bennie tromped the pedal and gripped the wheel, getting the Century's straight-eight to top eighty, the salesman at the car lot said it belonged to a guy who hardly drove it, fell on hard times and had to give it up, this one nearly two years old. Bennie flying along the 75. *Woohoo*, good old Buick." Slapping at the wheel, like she was a racehorse. The chassis holding nice and steady.

Heading back to the motel in Osage City, wanting to surprise Stella with it and take her for a spin, teach her to drive on these farm roads, thinking she'd ace it, same way she shot a gun. A heck of a girl.

And man, this sled could cook — three hundred and twenty cubic inch, a hundred and twenty horse — Bennie pushing it some more, flying over eighty now, the Century barely breaking a sweat.

Woohoo-ing again, just the best high-octane feeling in the world. "Old Clyde Barrow, you can keep your Ford, this baby's the real deal," Bennie yelled it out the open window, converting to a Buick man. Never drove anything finer, getting her up to seventy. That salesman telling it straight, this baby having the same engine as its big brother Roadmaster, told Bennie she'd top out at a hundred, if you had the stuff to hold on to the wheel — Bennie thinking he had the stuff alright — the salesman saying all you had to do was put your foot down and get a good road under her. Trouble was this wasn't that kind of road, just an empty stretch of gravel, potholes here and there, whipping by, but Bennie was in the mood to fly. Mashing his foot on the pedal, giving it everything. *Woohoo!*

Thinking about it after, he bet a tire snagged on one of those holes in the road, that or a big enough stone he didn't see, everything whizzing by at God's speed. He felt the bump, and he was wrestling the steering — trying to correct for the sway, oversteering and slamming a foot at the new hydraulic brakes, the second-best change the company made to her, the salesman told him.

Felt like the back end was floating for those few seconds, then she was screeching and humping on gravel, Bennie fighting that hard tug. Feeling it go in the air, launching over the shoulder and the ditch, his arms up and bracing, the Century leaping the ditch, taking a hard punch and plowing the undercarriage across the hardpan, going sideways, the dust of hell rising. He was rolling and the world was spinning. The grind of metal. Bennie was slammed around, head, hand and foot, and the carnival ride was over, Bennie spitting the sand from his mouth. Dust had him coughing, and he felt like he'd gone a few rounds with Barney Ross, punched and mauled from all sides.

Took a minute before he believed he was still in the world. Could be he blacked out, not sure how long he lay there. Bruised, but not busted, he crawled out the open window, scraped and bleeding, not a *woohoo* left in him, putting a hand on his knee, he forced himself upright, every part of him feeling a hundred years old and hurting like hell, his knees and elbows skinned, his ribs throbbing and his head pounding. Moving from the flipped-over car, its wheels in the air, laying on its crushed roof. Bennie hearing the drip of fluids and smelling gas. He was moving, so nothing was broken, felt a lump forming behind his ear, the pocket of his suit jacket flopping like the ear of a hound, Bennie getting dressed nice for when he walked in that dealership. Hoping the jacket could be mended. Wondering if Stella knew how to sew, maybe as good as she could shoot. Remembering his Colt that he shoved under the seat, he went back and looked around the dry ground for it, saw the gleam of steel and found it about twenty feet out front of the wreck, blew the sand from its cylinder, the pistol in need of a good cleaning.

A hard scramble to make it up the ditch, then he was looking back at the wreck, dead in the barren field, he'd never seen one in worse shape. Good as brand-spanking new the salesman had told him. Got spanked alright. It hurt to move, Bennie looking at the sky, saying, "Guess I should thank you, but how about we save it for later." Bennie angry with the world right then.

The county road stretched out in either direction, nobody around to witness how brainless a man could be. Not so much as a grasshopper, cricket or army-worm seeing Bennie hobbling on the road, favoring his right ankle. Anybody came along, he'd hitch his way back to Osage City, Stella likely to be wondering about him. No idea how he'd explain it to her. Paid for a car and walked back with nothing but a ripped pocket and a bunch of cuts and bruises, and forget going a few with Barney Ross, more like getting knocked around by the Manassa Mauler himself. Trudging for a couple of miles with the sun scorching down, and not a soul passing by to give him a lift.

(

He saw the car before he saw the diner — wasn't much more than a dusty shack, a sign called it Stoufer's Fine Eats. Another Buick was parked out front, not a Century, but an older Model 60, with its chrome grill grinning at him like it knew. If he wasn't hurting like a century-old man, he might have kicked a foot at its grinning grill.

Bennie pushed the screen door and stepped in the place. The woman behind the counter took him in and said he looked like he could use a cup.

"Sure wouldn't say no to one." Bennie swiped his hand at a fly, took a stool at the counter, eased himself on the vinyl. Asked her for a glass of water first, clearing his throat of sand before the coffee.

"You don't mind me asking, mister, you come off a rough night, or the day do this to you?" The middle-aged woman smiled at him, setting a glass and a cup in front of him.

"Ma'am, you got no idea." Thanking her for it, he finished the water, then took a sip of coffee — nothing ever better — his hand sweeping at the fly, asking, "That your Buick out front?"

"Could say so."

"Well, wondering if you'd be interested in selling her?"

"If it makes me a profit, I'd sell just about anything."

Sipping, he looked out at it. "A '32, 'less I miss my guess?"

"Guess you know your Buicks." The woman smiled, asking if he wanted something to eat.

"Love a good V8, though it tends to get me in trouble." Bennie shaking his head, saying he wasn't hungry.

"Well, it's got that, the big engine. You got a price in mind?" She watched him sip his coffee.

"Well, would need to take her for a test run, you understand, see what she's all about." Looking at the woman over his cup, blowing at it, hoping she'd fetch him the keys.

Mrs. Stoufer looked at him a moment longer, then turned to the kitchen pass-through and called for Fred to get out here. "Fella here interested in the car." Rolled her eyes, told Bennie Fred was her old man.

"We selling it?" Fred said, coming from the back, a bean-pole of a man with thick hair and a long neck, nodding to Bennie, untying a grease-covered apron and setting it on the counter.

"Depends what kind of offer this gent's got in mind." Mrs. Stoufer looked from the husband to Bennie, telling him the coffee was on the house.

Thanking her, Bennie said he was Robert Kane, then he followed behind Fred, taking the keys from him and climbing behind the wheel, Fred getting in on the passenger side.

Starting it up, Bennie said, "Sure got a nice purr to her."

Looking at him like he wasn't sure which "her" he meant, Fred said, "Yuh, guess she does."

"Had her a long time?"

"Got it baby-new and been a good car since. One a fella can depend on."

Driving back the way he had walked, Bennie passed the time of day, talking about the unending plague of weather, headlines in the news — how he read about Adolf Hitler having a sit-down with Neville Chamberlain, Fred saying he didn't care much about overseas, more interested in Miss Ohio making it to Miss USA — driving past the corpse of the Century about five miles down the road, its wheels skyward.

"Dumb kids out racing again," Fred said, shaking his head. "All that power and no idea what to do with it." Craning for a look as they passed, he crossed himself. "Don't see many wrecked worse than that, all crushed in."

"A shame, Century's one fine car. And this here one's none too bad either."

"Think we should have a look, maybe dumb kids are still inside?"

"Nobody's in it, and if they were, wouldn't be anything left to save, but I think you ought to tell me how much you're thinking, Fred?"

"Well, Robert, a new one'd run you, let's see, about a hard-earned twelve hundred, I believe. So, I reckon eight hundred's fair."

Bennie gave a soft whistle.

"Haven't run this one too hard, mostly to Topeka and back for supplies. Lot of life left in her, guess you can see that."

"Yeah, looks good, feels good, but eight's a bit steep, Fred. No offense." Slowing and coming to a stop in the road, Bennie said, "But what say I give you what I got on me, and owe you the rest?"

"Well, sir, that don't sound so good." Fred looking around, nothing but empty fields around them.

"Afraid it's the best I got to offer."

"You seem like a good fellow, Robert. But you can picture what the wife'll say — you met her, a strong woman — I come back with less than the full eight hundred . . ."

"I see what you mean, Fred. Here, maybe this'll help." Reaching behind his jacket, Bennie set the Colt in his lap, getting the expected reaction.

Fred staring at the barrel, his hands naturally going up.

Bennie saying, "I'm putting it this way 'cause I got no choice, and so we get an understanding between us." Then he took out what cash he had and counted it out. "Sorry it's got to be this way, I truly am, Fred. Can make it a hundred and twenty down, top of which I'm gonna send you the rest, the full eight hundred, plus an extra fifty to make up for your troubles, dealing with your missus and all. Here, go on and count it."

"When's that coming, the rest?"

"Soon's I get to the bank. And you got my word on it, okay?"

"Saying it like I got a choice."

"I wouldn't do it this way if I had another way to go." Thinking at least he'd be pulling up to the motel in a car, the one he told Stella he was going to buy.

"Well, sir, it's not like I got a choice in it." Fred reaching for the money and counting it.

"Wish I had a better way, but like I said, it's the best I can do. Now, I figure it's four, five miles back to your place. You look fit; you okay to walk it? See, I'm heading the other way."

"Guess I shouldn't be surprised." Fred looked back at the empty stretch of road, then at the pistol. "Guess it'll give me time to figure how I'm gonna put it to the missus."

Watching him get out, Bennie called out the window, "Stoufer's Diner, right? Where you want me to send your money?"

Fred waved a hand in the air and started walking.

... *seventeen*

SEPTEMBER 12, 1938

"Least you ain't gone and painted it yellow." Stella poking at him as soon as they were underway.

"Color's fine like it is, and told you I got a deal on it. Eight hundred and fifty bucks." Driving the seven hours north to Brookings, Bennie held back the story, feeling dumb for what happened. Knowing he couldn't hide the scrapes and bruises, set to tell her he tumbled down some stairs. And he meant what he told Fred Stoufer, about sending the money when they finished with the Brookings bank.

She brought it up again as they got closer to Kansas, about staying at her mother's.

"Been through it, lady, it's no time for getting misty-eyed. Already took a chance the one time. Too likely the cops'll be watching, and my folks' place too. Afraid it comes with the job."

"Not even a night?"

"Need to keep the law guessing left when we go right."

"Means we're sleeping in the car."

"Got a place in mind for tonight, called the City Tourist Camp. They got nice enough rooms, bunk beds and inside plumbing. If they got a phone, maybe you can make a call."

"Sounds lovey-dovey. I do believe you're getting misty-eyed, Johnny O'Malley. What's next, chocolates shaped like hearts?" Stella looking out at houses flying past.

"Won't set us back much, and a nice busy crossroads with easy access in case we got to high-speed it out of there."

"The perfect honeymoon spot. Or you forget you still owe me that?"

"Can't forget a thing when I'm always reminded of it." He grinned, tried to keep it light. "You crack me up, you know it?" No way he wanted to chance staying at her folks' place, one eye reciting Keats, the other keeping watch out the parlor window.

Stella knowing they were low on money because of the new car he bought, but thinking this wasn't much car for all that money, guessing there was more to the story; more to the story about him tumbling down some stairs too. Favoring his ankle, the scrape and bruises, and the torn jacket. Saying, "Guess we'd be staying in a better place, except with you playing squirrel, hiding the money at your folks' farm." Stella never liked that he buried it, not showing her the exact spot.

"Well, I can't put it in a bank, can I?"

"Not the way them places get robbed."

Both of them laughed, then went quiet a while, both staring ahead out the windshield.

Stella saying, "So, now what? More fights?"

"Told you, I got something cooking."

"That bank again, the one in Brookings." She said it, not asking it like a question.

"Northwest Security. I mean, if you want to stay in nice

places, 'less you don't mind sleeping in that old boxcar till I get my studies done. No running water and digging a hole for a toilet there though."

She made a face.

"And this bank's a honey, I tell you. Gonna make enough on it, never need to do it again. Had my eye on it that day you went shopping."

"Same day as the Elkton bank." She rolled her eyes. "When you were supposed to be helping me pick out a birthday present, help me get the size right."

"Best birthday ever, you said."

"I'm not complaining about it." Stella slid close and leaned against his shoulder, asking, "When?"

"End of next month, harvest time, such as it is. Be more deposits then."

Sitting upright and giving him a look. "That enough time?"

"Already planned it." He tapped his temple. "Where'd you think I was when you were baking pies with my momma?"

"You said fishing."

"You see any fish?"

"Just thought you were bad at it."

"You think I can't fish?"

"I bet you can do anything." She put her hands to his cheeks and turned his head and kissed him, kept him from seeing the road again.

"Not gonna start that again." Giving her a gentle nudge back, saying, "You want to send us right in that ditch and wreck the car? Smarten up now."

"Thought you liked it dangerous."

"Like it 'cause it's you. Sometimes soft is good, and there's a bed at the tourist camp."

She sat back, giving up on it, saying, "So, tell me about this bank."

"About five thousand or so folks live there, a lot of them favoring the Northwest Security, an easy getaway spot at Taylor's Corner, heart of the shopping district. Town'll be celebrating Hobo Day, like a homecoming parade or something. Be banners and posters all over."

"And it'll be Halloween." She got a look of concern. "You're not gonna make us wear straw hats and overalls again?"

"Going in different. Don't want them tying it to the one in Elkton."

"Dressing up fancy?" She brightened.

"That's right. Gonna wear my suit and these eyeglasses." Reaching them off the dash, showing them to her. "Gonna pomade my hair and wear a hat. You in your new outfit."

"Showing some style."

"And we're going in first thing when it's quiet, looking like customers, right when it opens. Only be the manager and a couple tellers then. Be out in five minutes."

"I'm not waiting by the car again, I can tell you that much."

"You didn't the last time either, supposed to watch and whistle."

"You were taking so long. Plus I can't whistle worth spit."

"Understand why you did it, but we got to be of a mind on this. We plan it, we got to stick to it."

She nodded.

"You go in with that new green dress and that nice coat and shoes. Stand in the lobby with your eye on the door, the pistol in your pocket."

"Thought you liked the black one?"

Smiling at her. "Guess you think it's like going to a fancy ball."

"I know what it is. What I want to know is the car story you don't want to tell."

"Makes you think there's a car story?"

"'Cause I can feel it."

"Guess I can't keep anything from you."

"Nope, you can't," she said, waiting for him to tell her what happened.

But he didn't, saying instead, "We got enough for the tourist camp. And soon going to have plenty more. Top of which, we won't be walking in the bank looking like a couple of wrecks this time. All you need to know."

. . . *eighteen*

OCTOBER 31, 1938

"Don't want to start sweating in this, get stains on the silk," Stella said, meaning the green dress, glad it wasn't all wrinkled from being folded in the trunk. "And these things are pinching my toes."

"I like the shoes, and the boys'll all be looking at the shape of your calves. Keep them from picking you from a line-up."

"Well, I like not going in like hobos." Stella looking at the banners up across the street, Brookings celebrating Hobo Day, still hanging from last Saturday.

Behind the wheel of the black coupe he stole, Bennie was getting his head in the game, driving around the corner of the bank, Taylor's Corner quiet at this hour. Glancing at the front door between the long columns. Driving past, saying, "You see it?"

"Yeah, it's something."

"Meant the clothes shop next door. Too bad it's closed."

"You're a funny man."

Pulling around the block, getting back onto Fourth, he stopped along the tall windows down the side of the building, saying they'd wait till it opened.

"Shame the clothes shop ain't — open, I mean."

"Could pop the lock for you."

"Give me something to do, keep me from getting the jitters."

The two of them smiling, looking at each other. Neither wanting to let their nerves show.

Pulling down the visor, she drew on the lipstick, the brick wall of the bank on her right. Her hand shook enough, and she was surprised she could do it without making a mess. Looking in the dark windows, telling herself it would be alright. The two of them would always be alright. Liz and her friends at school had talked about catching a good one, back when she was part of that group, before that man gave her that ride from hell, Stella having to undergo those awful treatments, the whole town finding out and dealing with her like she had the plague.

But here she was, married to Bad Bennie Dickson, and her luck had taken a change. Stella guessing those schoolgirls would end up with farming men and garage mechanics, men with working hands, coming home at the end of a sweaty day, dog-tired from doing the kind of work that hurried them into old age. Bennie wasn't the kind to take the crumbs of life. More the kind to reach for the whole pie, and not afraid to take it. And he'd always look out for her. Funny thinking about the future and her rest-of-days like this, and here she was, just turned sixteen two months back.

"We got time yet," he said. "What say to breakfast, drugstore looks open, looks like they got a counter, bacon and eggs, maybe flapjacks?" Nodding across the street, the lit sign saying the place was Tidball's.

"I can't think about eating right now." Stella lifted the visor.

"Most important meal of the day is what they say. Could sit by the window, give us a chance to scope the bank, see who comes and who goes."

"Maybe a coffee then." She was reaching the door handle when a man, about Bennie's age, came from the front of the bank, wearing a dark suit and stepping between the pillars, going past them and crossing to the drugstore. He was whistling a tune.

"You see that, the man doesn't have a care in the world," he said. "Hold on, I got an idea."

"Gonna get him to teach me to whistle?"

Taking the glasses from the dash, he slipped them on, said it wasn't a bad idea. Getting out, he went around and leaned on the passenger door and tapped on her window. When she rolled it down, Bennie made like he was passing the time, showing his own whistle, telling her, "Put your lips like this and just blow, see?" Watching the fellow in the dark suit coming from Tidball's drugstore, waiting for a passing car, then crossing the street. Bennie saying to her, "Think we'll get rain today, lady?"

"Rain, are you nuts? Can't remember what it looks like. But you're just talking about nothing, shooting the breeze, just want me nodding my head, huh, like what you got to say's something smart?"

"That's right, lady." Bennie grinned, hoping the breeze was all he'd shoot that day. Looking at the fellow in the dark suit cutting across the street, still whistling with a soda bottle in his hand.

"Sure early for soda pop," Bennie said as he passed.

"Yeah, used to be coffee, but it gets me jumping." Reaching in a pocket, pulling out a ring of keys, the banker went to the corner, calling behind him. "And she's sure a beaut — the car, I mean." Nodding and smiling at Stella.

"Nice of you to say." Waiting till he turned, Bennie opened the back door and reached in for the sawed-down shotgun, told Stella to wait a couple of minutes, then pull the car out front by the pillars. Taking a last look around, he followed the man between the pillars, holding the sawed-down shotgun along his right leg. Hearing the man whistling ahead of him.

"Won't be open till nine, I'm afraid, mister." The man was fumbling and jingling the ring of keys, aware of Bennie, but not looking past his shoulder. "Darn things all look alike."

"Yeah, well, I was hoping you can help me out. I got this banknote I need to get tended," Bennie said, taking the three steps up between the pillars.

Fitting the key in the lock, the man turned the doorknob, saying over his shoulder, "Banknote's no problem, I mean if you got an account with us."

Touching the short barrel to the man's back, Bennie pushed him inside, shut the door behind him and spun the man around. "Think you can make an exception."

The man held his hands wide, scared, understanding what was happening, his eyes fixed on the barrels.

"Your name, bet you got one?"

"John, John Torsey." Standing frozen, the bottle dangling from his fingers.

"Well, John Torsey, you go on and sip your soda. I just need you to help me make a withdrawal. You understand that, and there won't be no trouble."

John Torsey nodded.

"Okay, let's go and meet the staff, get some help opening the drawers and that vault you got in back."

"Uh uhn, not the vault."

"Am I talking to the wrong man, John?" Bennie pressed the barrel at his stomach.

"Just saying it's got a time lock."

"You kidding me?" Bennie couldn't believe it, looked around for someplace to complain. Thinking a moment, then saying, "Okay, we go in like nothing's happened."

Past the low saloon-type doors, they turned right, Bennie holding the gun along his leg. Taking in the employees working past a partition, a shadow of a man in an office behind a glass door, a woman at a desk in the public area, and another man with graying hair behind the cashier's counter. The graying man gave them a passing glance, going to a check-posting machine, looking up again and asking, "I help you, sir?" Late seeing the shotgun, partly hidden by the partition.

Lifting it and letting him see it, Bennie asked his name.

Said he was Curtis Lovre, holding his hands wide.

"Well, Curtis, you see what I got here?"

The man nodded.

The woman looked up from her desk, and Bennie nudged John Torsey ahead of him, telling him to have a seat across from her, motioned Curtis from the check-posting machine. Everybody taking a seat, looked like a meeting. Setting the shotgun on top of the desk, next to Dorothy Coffey's nameplate. Taking the Colt from behind his back, he put it in front of him and said, "I appreciate you acting natural, can you do that, Dorothy?"

Her lip trembled and she started to cry, saying, "I'm sorry. It's my first time."

"You're gonna do fine, just got to hear what I say to you, okay?"

She nodded again.

The glass door to the office opened, an older gent stepped out, his name in gold letters on the glass: Richard M. DePuy, asking what he was paying them all for, then seeing the shotgun, the color quick leaving his face.

"You go by Dick or Richard?" Bennie said.

DePuy's mouth dropped open, looked like he might speak, but no words came out.

John Torsey offered up, "He goes by Richard, hates being called Dick."

"Okay then, Richard it is," Bennie said, "and just so you folks understand, your lives are in your own hands. One acts the wrong way, and you're all in it. Now, I'm not looking to do you harm, but I want you being clear on it." Looking at each one, he said, "I just want what's in those drawers." Winking at Dorothy. "Now, if you can pull yourself together, ma'am, I'd be obliged if you empty them for me. Think you can do it?"

She nodded and started to rise, tears wetting her cheeks.

"And if you got an alarm in this place, I'd appreciate you not tripping it." Bennie looked at Richard DePuy, saying, "Never shot anybody before, and sure hate to start this day off the wrong way." Pulling a flour sack he had stuffed in a pocket, he handed it to Dorothy. "You need to dry your eyes, feel free to use the corner."

She did, drying her eyes, then stepping to the cash drawers and getting to work.

"And Dorothy, leave some small bills, huh, enough to do business, in case somebody comes in." Then to the three men: "Remember, boys, all this money's insured. Not yours to get killed over."

All three nodded.

A knock at the front door, and Bennie turned and said to John Torsey, "If that's a pretty blonde, you may as well let her in." Wagging the barrel, he pointed to the door.

Her heels sounded on the floor, Stella came in and took the pistol from her open coat pocket, Bennie telling her to keep an eye on Dorothy and Curtis. Then saying to Richard DePuy and John Torsey, "Let's go see that vault." Tucking the pistol in his belt, he picked up the shotgun, following them to the back, into the darkened vault room, Torsey reaching for a light cord.

Putting the barrel on him, Bennie said, "Pull it if you want, John, but anything but a light comes on, yours is going out, you understand me?"

Nodding, John Torsey tugged the cord, illuminating a small safe in the vault room, and the large steel door painted black, built into the far wall. Bennie looked at the smaller safe, saying to him, "How about that one?"

Torsey said he knew the combination, gave a nervous look to DePuy, knelt by it and spun the dial, pulling back the door.

Taking out a second flour sack, Bennie handed it to him, and Torsey filled it, counting as he did, handing it back, saying, "About two thousand there."

"I appreciate it, John." Turning to Richard DuPuy, Bennie said, "Bet you being manager, you can get us past that time lock."

"Afraid you'd be wrong, gun or no gun, nobody on earth's going to open it till exactly ten thirty." Looking smug about it, saying, "Not even our eager Mr. Torsey can do anything about it." Frowning at the bank employee, DePuy smiled at Bennie, like that was it, nothing he could do about it.

"Well, then, guess we'll just wait."

"Wait? You can't wait."

"Why you people keep saying that? You expect me to make an appointment, come back at a time that suits you?"

"I expect you to know when a thing's done, is all," DePuy said. "No offense, mister, but it's just not going to work out for you."

"Well, sir, how about you let me worry about it." Motioning the two from the vault room.

"You stick around and every lawman in town'll be outside those doors by the time the safe pops," John Torsey said. "Just can't get away with it."

"And I thank you for looking out for me, John. Either way, like I said, we're gonna find out." Bennie went and looked out at the main room, where Stella was pacing back and forth, looking nervous. He took out the pocket watch. One minute ahead of nine.

He wanted them to carry on with the bank's business, Bennie warning about doing anything suspect, told them what would happen if anybody looked the wrong way or tried passing a customer a note. Bennie taking a position behind the counter, close to DePuy's office, keeping an eye on the goings-on. Laying the shotgun along a middle shelf, in easy reach. The pistol behind his back, under his jacket. "If anybody asks, I'm a bank inspector, on top of you." He looked at DePuy, saying, "Here on official business."

Sitting on a chair in the lobby, the .38 under a folded news-paper, Stella made like she was waiting on an appointment.

The hour and a half crawled by, felt like a week, Bennie counting nearly fifty heads coming through the doors — no way he could make them all lie on the floor like he did in Elkton. Playing bank inspector, he leaned on the counter next to DePuy's office, smiling as Dorothy and Curtis cashed banknotes, helping customers with deposits and with-drawals, one fellow coming in twice. Bennie keeping an eye on that man cashing a note, then coming back a half hour later to change a large bill. Bennie's sweaty hand stayed near the shotgun under the counter, the barrel lined with DePuy's belly, watching the banker approve a loan for a young couple. Bennie telling them to have a nice day when they left.

A tall man walked in, asking DePuy about catching a coffee break, DePuy telling the man he was having a son-of-a-gun day, with the inspector here, saying tomorrow would be better. Passing the time, Bennie had Dorothy Coffey show him to the security-deposit boxes, getting her to open each one, looking them over, not finding much of interest.

Standing next to him at the security boxes, she leaned close, trying to hide her face, saying in a low voice her sister just entered the bank, said she'd never fool her, asking to be excused to powder her nose, promising to do it without foolishness. Nodding to Stella, Bennie had her escort Dorothy to the ladies' room in back, the two of them coming back out after the sister cashed a check and left, the two chatting about the dress shop next door, talking hemlines and floral prints.

Twenty minutes to go, Bennie shook the watch, thinking maybe it stopped again, didn't matter it was Swiss. With no customers in the bank right then, he asked Curtis, "That yours?" Looking at a topcoat on a wooden rack.

"Yeah, just got it."

"How much, if you don't mind me asking?"

"Was twenty-five bucks, from a place in Kansas City. Same place I bought the suit." Looking down at it.

"Real nice." Bennie touched the fabric of the coat, asked if Curtis minded if he tried it on, then said, "What say I buy it from you?"

"Buy it?"

"Yeah, I don't get much shopping time these days, and we look about the same size, you and me. What say I give you the twenty-five, plus a couple extra. Can go shop yourself a new one, something I won't get to do."

"I see what you mean. Well, yeah, I guess that'd be alright."

"Go and take twenty-five from the cash drawer. That all right with you, Mr. DePuy?"

Richard DePuy shook his head like he couldn't believe it — Bennie trying on the coat, the pistol showing behind his back — then he sighed and nodded.

"Not gonna do something miserable, like make him pay it back the minute I go out the door, are you?" Bennie said.

"I think the man's been through enough," DePuy said. "The coat's yours, consider it bought and paid for."

At ten thirty, Bennie took one of the part-filled sacks and moved Richard DePuy and Curtis Lovre to the vault room, saying, "Sure hope this thing pops before I do." Pointing the shotgun, and grabbing the steel handle, finding it still locked.

"Sometimes it takes a minute or so extra," Curtis said.

Ordering Curtis to check for any silver pieces they'd missed from the small safe, Bennie stared at the lock like he was willing it to open. Finally, hearing it click, he sucked a breath, handing the flour sack to Curtis. Putting his back to the door while the banker stuffed it full. More money than Bennie had ever seen in one place in his life. Then following them back into the main room, he told Dorothy to clear the cash drawers, thanking her for doing a fine job, stuffing the bills in his pockets, and tucking the pistol out of sight, Bennie taking his new coat and draping it over the shotgun, holding it low.

"Be a good fellow now, and take it out to my car." Bennie got the door for Curtis and let Stella go first. Too much for just Lovre to carry on his own, Richard DePuy helped him carry the stuffed sack out past the pillars, out to the Buick. Bennie carrying the smaller sack in one hand, the shotgun in the other, Stella coming behind him.

Turning at the door, Bennie wished Dorothy Coffey and John Torsey a nice day, said he didn't expect it, but he'd appreciate a five-minute head start — both of them bobbing their heads. Then Bennie was looking past the pillars, going to the car where Stella had parked it. Opening the passenger door for her, he laid the coat and shotgun on the floor behind the seat, next to a box of roofing nails and the old suitcase holding their clothes. Then going to the driver's side.

A green Plymouth pulled into the spot next to the stolen coupe, a weathered farmer parking too close, making it impossible for DePuy and Lovre to open the passenger door and shove the sack past the seat to the rear cargo area. Oblivious, the farmer slid across his bench seat and got out his passenger door.

"Hey, mister, you mind, you parked us in?" Bennie called to him.

Hard of hearing and not looking back, the man kept walking into the bank, going between the pillars. Bennie told the bankers to shove it in on the driver's side, the two men carrying the sack around and squeezing it in the cargo area behind the seat. Then he told DePuy and Lovre to step up on the running boards, and Bennie and Stella got in. He laid the pistol on the seat, waiting for the bankers to step onboard, saying, "Hold tight, fellas, till I say jump."

A sedan from the twenties slowed and stopped behind his bumper, blocking them in, Bennie grabbing for his pistol, thinking it was the law. Realizing it was an elderly woman stepping out the passenger door, bending in and saying so long to the driver, leaning on a cane, saying something about the driver not hanging around the bar and being late for supper.

Getting out and going to the driver's window, Bennie tapped on the glass and explained to the old-timer behind the wheel that he was blocking him in. The old-timer looked doubtful, taking his time opening his door and getting out of the Plymouth, said he'd been driving longer than Bennie had been alive.

"Yeah, I bet you're right," Bennie said, seeing the old woman leaning on her cane and hobbling up the bank's steps. Bennie was hoping Dorothy Coffey and John Torsey were giving him that five-minute head start.

"You say I hit you, son? Show me where." The old man was concerned, bending and squinting for damage.

"Didn't say you hit me, I said you got us boxed in. Just asking can you move it?" Bennie clung on to his cool, saying, "You want, I'll be happy to do it for you, mister."

"I told you, I been driving since you were a pup. What makes you think you can do it better'n me?"

"Just mean I can do it faster."

"The trouble with young people, always rushing." Ready for a squabble, the old fellow was slow getting back behind the wheel, grinding it in gear and rolling past the spot, muttering to himself.

Asking the bankers to get back up on the running boards, Bennie backed out, his pistol in his lap, shotgun on the seat, he rolled south on Main, Curtis Lovre and Richard DePuy hanging on for dear life — no sign of the law — and Bennie swung the turn, going east on Third, using the bankers like shields. Couldn't risk driving into a police ambush like Clyde Barrow had done.

Rolled a couple of blocks past townsfolk looking on, one woman waving like maybe it was part of the Hobo Day parade. Bennie slowed out front of the courthouse, telling DePuy and Lovre to jump off, thanking them, then he sped off. Stella Mae smiling out the back window, blowing them a kiss.

Pulling around the block, he drove slower than he wanted through Brookings, then out to U.S. 14, heading in the direction of the Dicksons' farm, thirty miles to the east, to another abandoned cropper's shack Bennie knew about.

Wanting to count the money, knowing it was a big score. His mind was racing, thinking about painting this Buick some other color, or maybe he'd just steal another one, maybe go for a Ford again.

"Well, that went smooth, nearly to plan," Bennie said.

"You kidding, I almost had a kitten, those goddamn locks," she said, throwing her arms around his neck, then kissing him, glad to be alive. Saying, "So, how much you figure?" Looking over the seat at the stuffed flour sack.

"Didn't exactly take the time to count it, lady, but it's sure more than we got in Elkton."

Stella leaned across and kissed him again, Bennie stopping her from climbing back in his lap. Told her to save that stuff for later.

. . . nineteen

NOVEMBER 22, 1938

Stretching his back muscles, feeling tight from the four-hour drive that started in Detroit, he took them through Battle Creek and Kalamazoo. Driving like he was never going to stop, this ninety-mile-an-hour Plymouth he stole, passing fifty-mile-an-hour drivers on a forty-mile-an-hour road. Blowing by some crawling Edsel, the driver taking his half of the road out of the middle, Bennie passing on the shoulder.

Stopped for gas and sandwiches at a roadside stand, Bennie telling Stella to get set for the best ginger ale in the world. Stella admitting it was pretty good, looking at the bottle of Vernor's. The Swiss on rye wasn't bad either.

Bennie had driven north to buy a couple of cars, built some new aliases in Michigan, creating a false trail. Now he was heading west, planning to go south, wind their way back to New Orleans, where they'd been hiding. Stella falling in love with the place, the food, the music and the warmer weather.

"They got cars in Kansas, you know?" she said. "And we can make up names anyplace."

"We're throwing the lawmen off the trail, you know that. Anybody they ask gives the names we left behind and points them the wrong way." Bennie always feeling they were being hunted, and right now he was trying to steer her out of the dark mood she'd been in since he drove through Michigan, guessing it was because they were this close to her mother's place and he wasn't going to swing by. Being patient with her, saying, "Besides, there're more cars in Detroit than anyplace else, and along with some nice sights."

"Sights? Name one thing was worth seeing?"

"Well, you liked the shops on Woodward Avenue. And the Packard factory. How about the electric streetcars, you never seen them before, and said you liked that bridge all the way to Canada."

"Big deal, Canada."

"Well, I'm hoping that's where they think we've gone. Plus you got in some shopping when I got the cars. Seemed to be having a good time."

She had to admit to that, buying a couple more dresses and pairs of shoes. Picked out a herringbone suit for him, replaced the one he ripped in the crash back in Osage City. Surprised him with a two-tone pair of city shoes to go with it. Telling him if he was going to be on the run, he ought to do it in style, like his hero John Dillinger, the man always doing his bloody business in a nice suit.

Driving what he called his fresh Pontiac, he left a dark brown Buick he bought in a rented garage in Highland Park, just in case they needed it sometime. Bennie seeing the sign now for Crown Point, Indiana, fives miles ahead, putting them just south of Chicago. He took out the folded paper, a hand-drawn map he'd made before they left Detroit that morning. "Know what I said about it, but I guess the only thing's gonna put a smile back on your face is if we stop in at your mother's." Bennie giving in.

She lit up and practically jumped off the seat, looking at him. "You mean it?"

"Why'd I say it if I didn't mean it."

And she threw her arms around his neck and was kissing him.

"Now come on, don't start that again."

"You don't want me to?"

"Want you to remember it for later." And he pecked her cheek, smiling at her.

It took him a while to find what he was looking for, weaving through city streets, finally pulling up in front of a red brick building, a long porch across the one end, and he said, "Here we go — surprise!"

"What's this place?" She looked at it, nothing special about it.

"The jail where Dillinger made his famous escape."

"We sightseeing again?"

"Must've told you about it, his '34 escape, one that made all the papers."

"Guess I missed it." She looked at it, rolled her eyes so he couldn't see, saying it looked nice enough, thinking it sure wasn't worth driving for hours.

"They called it escape-proof. That's all you had to tell a guy like John Dillinger, and he set out to prove you wrong. And he did it too, got out of there, and made it look easy as pie."

"Yeah, how'd he do it?" Stella sighed, taking in the brick building that looked more like a city hall than a jail.

"Did it with a wooden pistol, one he carved and painted with shoe polish, and through his own channels, paid to have a car waiting outside." Looking at her, he smiled. "But there's another reason I brought you here."

"For a second, I was afraid you were gonna give yourself up and break out of jail, do it for good old John Dillinger."

"Just wanted to see it one time, is all. Make fun all you want, but the guy was the ace."

"Dillinger?"

"Yeah, the best in the business."

"Better'n you?"

"Two banks against two dozen. What do you think?"

"Think maybe you need to go see somebody?"

"Yeah, joke if you want, but the fact is we're both going to see somebody. The other reason we're here, this historic spot — to mark the special occasion."

"Going to turn us both in?"

He turned on the seat as best he could with the steering column in the way, the prison in the background. Contorting to get to one knee, he reached in a pocket, taking out a small box and holding it out.

"What's this. You crazy, how many times you want to marry me?"

"Well, one time I asked you to be Mrs. Bennie Dickson, sometimes Mrs. Johnny O'Malley. And this time, I'm asking you to be Mrs. James Duncan, maiden name of Elva Clayton." The names they made up and used around Detroit.

"So, let me get this, you want to marry me, this time as Elva. You and me using names that ain't ours because you're hoping to throw off the law? Why Johnny, or Bennie, or James, you're the biggest romantic I ever saw."

"And I'm hoping you'll say yes. Pretty soon too, on account sitting like this is cramping me awful."

"You're a nut, Mr. James Duncan, you know it?" Taking the ring from the box, looking at it, and slipping it on.

"So can I take that as a yes?"

. . . *twenty*

NOVEMBER 24, 1938

Sitting in the rocker outside the Ace Motor Court room, Bennie kept an eye on the busy crossroads with easy access in case they had to race out of there, cars and trucks going by. Flapping open the paper, he found the article on page three. The *Daily Capital* running another piece on the Brookings job, bank bookkeeper Dorothy Coffey giving her account of what happened nearly a month ago. Calling through the screen door, he read it aloud: "Calling us the time-lock bandits, a couple of Robin Hood incidents the way we handled it."

"A couple of what?"

"Talks about me buying that man Curtis's coat and paying with the bank's own money — guess that's why. And it goes on about me keeping my head, playing it cool, middle of the holdup, how not a shot got fired."

"Say anything about me, the way I handled it, or how I was dressed?"

Bennie laughed, getting a kick from the piece, yawning in spite it being two in the afternoon, not used to being up most of the night, drinking and having a good time. "Just says we take from the rich and give to the poor."

"That make me Maid Marian?" Stella thinking, shit, another alias. Realizing she was in a fair mood for a change, having seen her mother and stepdad last night. Didn't tell her parents she got married again under a new name, too much to try and explain in a short time. Took Hattie and Lester for a ride in the Plymouth. Then, leaving it behind the house, Bennie borrowed the family's Pontiac and took Stella and her friend Liz Musick to a late supper, a nice place called the Sunset Inn, not far from the local police station. Bennie taking a chance being spotted. It was pot roast night, and Bennie sat mopping gravy with his biscuits, keeping an eye out the window while Stella and Liz caught up.

Then they'd gone to the Oasis nightclub, the two girls talking like it was old times, staying out half the night, and half-drunk coming back to the camp after two. Bennie being a good sport about it, hiding his yawns while the girls kept catching up.

"Don't knock it," Bennie called inside. "That Maid Marian was some dish, like in that movie you want to see, Olivia de Havilland playing her." Bennie chuckled and kept reading, saying, "Oh, here you go, right at the end, calls you a pleasing blonde with a deadly look. Walking back and forth, a gun moll armed with a big pistol, like you were daring anybody to come in and try something. What do you think of that?"

"Think they're talking about somebody else."

"Calls me Bad Bennie with nerves of steel, hanging around an hour and a half for that time lock to pop, getting away with seventeen thousand and five ninety-three, plus another sixteen thousand in securities. Not a bad day's pay."

"If you don't mind it leading to a lifetime of running."

"The running'll be over soon. Oh, and they got an eyewitness called Chenowith, one who came in and had DePuy renew a note. Says old Dick did his job, all the while with the glum and armed fugitive trying to pass as a bank inspector, that being yours truly, keeping a deadly watch, what he calls it. You figure I got that, a deadly watch?"

"You got your moments. Called you Bad Bennie, huh? So they know who we are?"

"Doesn't mention you by name, says Chenowith describes me as five eight or so, you as regular, about a hundred and twenty or so pounds, with eyes of steel blue."

"What's that mean, regular? Well, I guess he got the eyes right, but I never been a hundred and twenty in my life. Ought to call them and clear it up."

Bennie laughed again, saying, "Maybe being on the run takes off the pounds — you know, a way for a girl to keep trim."

"So they tied the two banks, and they know who we are?"

"Just mentions me as Bad Bennie, likely on account of my past." Bennie looked in at her past the screen, never thought much about his folks seeing the papers, getting a sick feeling about it now: his father reading it in the *Daily Capital*. Then he was saying, "A few weeks back we're sleeping in a stolen car hidden in a barn, near out of money, now we're sitting pretty again. Just got to relax and look forward, and not back." He was thinking he ought to bury some more of the money, like he had done with the securities, hid them by the old railcar Spencer had dubbed Ben's cabin. Holding back a few grand as walking-around money, he ought to bury the rest of the cash, come back and get it when he needed it. Not liking that some was sitting in the flour sack in the trunk, the rest in the suitcase.

Then she was behind him, looking out through the mesh.

"Guess maybe I just like reading about myself." He folded the paper, dropped it on the stoop, took out his watch and checked the time. "Well, what say we put some miles between us and here?"

"Already got us packed." The new suitcase with their belongings stood behind her: their new clothes, ammunition, the letters he'd written her from California. Stella wishing he'd leave the money packed in a suitcase too, hated that he wanted to bury more of it. She'd feel better having it close.

Pushing himself up, feeling a hundred years old from last night's drinking, he arched his back and drew a breath, feeling that throb in his side, same one that had dogged him since the crash back in Osage City. And he was getting stiff sitting in cars lately, not working out in a boxing gym. Opening the screen door, keeping it ajar with a foot, he reached in and lifted the suitcase, surprised by the weight, saying, "Man, you been shopping again?" And he backed out, bum butting the screen door.

"Put 'em up, Ben Dickson. We got you!"

"Get down." Bennie's eyes met hers, and he took a slow turn, and he set down the suitcase, his hands coming up slow, eyes down on the steps. The shadows of men moving in front and to his left. Sizing things up, Bennie jumped off the porch, dodging right and running down the side of the cabin, racing for the garage, voices shouting for him to stop. His feet were piston-pounding when the first shot ripped past him, a zip like the sound of a hornet. Hoping Stella listened this once, he threw himself past the cracked-open garage door. A volley of shots poured into the garage, pocking holes in the boards, hitting the Plymouth, filling the place with dust. Down on the earth floor, he fumbled with the key, bullets striking sheet metal.

Opening the car door, he pulled himself in, stayed down and cranked it. The engine fired, then stalled. Bennie cursing it, cranking the key again, saying, "Come on, baby." The engine springing to life amid the popping of gunfire, shards of wood and debris flying through the air.

He raised his head above the dash, enough to see out. Holes pocked the boards, daylight streaming in, a shotgun blast ripped a gash a man could slip through. The car shook, Bennie coughing and shoving the gas pedal with his hand, feeling lead tearing into the car's body, pinging off the metal, glass breaking.

Past the open door, one of the shadows lobbed something, a tear-gas grenade bouncing off the door, the smoke blowing back at the lawmen. Giving him his chance. Rising up and jamming the transmission to reverse, he hit the gas and braced, smashing through the back, splintering the boards, ramming into the office behind the cabin, crumpling the car's bumper. Cranking the wheel, he dropped low and drove blind between the cabins, bouncing off the cladding, another shotgun blast taking out the rear window. Bouncing off another cabin, he hoped Stella had climbed out a back window. No chance of turning around for her.

And he was on Topeka Avenue, looking back, hoped he'd see her running. Then he was driving past the cruisers the cops had left outside the Ace Motor Court grounds, bouncing off the door of the first one, his car shaking and rattling as he drove off, one wheel wobbling. Looking in the rearview for Stella.

(

As soon as he yelled for her to get inside, she grabbed into her bag for the .38. Lawmen were yelling outside, followed by gunshots. Rushing to the window, she caught sight of Bennie running for the garage. The highway patrolmen were chasing him, firing as he disappeared past the open garage doors. One rushing with a shotgun and blasting through the boards. The others with their pistols, every man aiming and firing into that garage.

She stopped herself from yelling "No!" She raised the pistol to shoot at them, then one of them lobbed a canister in an underhand swing, tried to get it through the garage doors. Bouncing off the door, the tear gas blew and pushed the men back, temporarily stopping the gunfire. She heard the engine cough to life, then heard the crashing, knowing what it meant, knowing he was alive.

And she was out the door, picking the suitcase off the steps — all the men facing the other way — and she hurried around the cabin's corner, and she was going through the lane of the camp, moving like she was late getting to the market, just saw herself making it to the trees beyond. Hearing his voice in her head, telling her to walk, not run, nobody was looking at her.

Folks stepped from their doors, sticking their heads out, wondering what was going on. "Maybe some kind of back-firing," she said to one woman, the woman nodding like that made sense.

Allowing herself one glance back, Stella felt her heart punch like it might come through her chest. One of the uniformed cops was coming behind her, hurrying like he wanted to catch up. Slipping her hand into her coat pocket, she kept walking from the motor court grounds, heading for the riverbank beyond it.

And he was calling to her now, telling her to stop. She kept going, like she didn't hear him, then he was closer and he called again. And she kept on, moving along the brush and weeds, walking upstream along the bank of Soldier Creek. Telling herself she could do this.

The cop called again for her to stop, warned that he'd shoot a woman just the same.

Setting down the suitcase, she took a couple more steps, stopped and turned, drawing the pistol from her coat pocket, keeping it at her side, but letting him see it. His sidearm still in its flapped holster.

She clicked off the safety and kept looking at him.

His eyes were round with fear, only had a couple of years on her. Nobody was backing him up, coming from behind him. The young cop on his own, and she just stared at him, waiting for him to make up his mind.

Seemed to take forever, then he took a step and reached for the suitcase she had set down.

She tried to tell him to put it down, but her words wouldn't come, she raised her pistol, aiming it at him, and her hand was shaking.

Doing it slow, he picked it up, then he turned and walked back the way he came, never looking back. Still aiming at his back, she watched him go past the reeds, then lost sight of him before she turned and kept going along the bank the opposite way, running when she could over the uneven ground. Not stopping until she saw bridge girders, must have run a couple of miles.

Pacing, finally huddling in her coat under that bridge, drawing her knees under her, she shuddered and kept the pistol next to her on the ground. The river rolling lazy and bubbling brown next to her. Putting her arms around herself as the day gave way to the chill of evening, nothing to do but shiver and cry in the November cold. Pulling her coat around her, drifting into an uneasy sleep, awoken by the sound of men up on the bridge. Moving for a look, she saw them silhouetted up there with their lanterns and rifles, searching for her.

The cold bit deeper, and she shook and thought about Bennie, praying he got away, out there somewhere in the night, leading the lawmen on a chase heading from Topeka, drawing them away from her. Guessing he'd switch cars and circle back. Remembering what he told her: if they got separated, she was to meet up with him at this abandoned shack he'd shown her on a map he drew, this place up in Iowa.

Sixteen years old and police and government men wanted to shoot her. Didn't even know her. Men acting like it was their own money. Taking it personal.

Bennie had signed William and Estelle Harrison on the motor court's register, the lawmen tracking them in spite of the aliases. Maybe somebody tipped them off, recognized them from some newspaper picture.

At first light she left the safety of the bridge, crossed a barren field, her heels scraping the hard earth, nothing growing on account of the ten years of drought, the Plains more dead than alive, what they called the badlands. God must have a dislike for this place, and a scorn for the folks who tried to survive on it. One thing she agreed with God about, she didn't care much for it either. She wanted to be back in New Orleans or out on the coast, where everything was growing green, with plenty of water, and the earth was black and rich, not all cracked and dead.

. . . twenty-one

NOVEMBER 25, 1938

Hitching a ride, somewhere near Hoyt, she watched the old Dodge pickup with a couple of wood barrels in the bed slowing and pulling to a grinding stop on the lonely two-lane. The truck was a mix of faded brown paint and rust, maybe one time it had been red. A rifle on a rack sat in the rear window. Two scruffy men in flannel and over-alls looking her over and telling her to jump in. The one on the passenger side getting out, his belly poking through his shirt buttons. Telling her to slide between them, rubbing his scruffy chin, giving her a bad feeling. "Where you heading, darlin'?"

"North. And how about I just hop in back. Don't want to crowd you gents."

"How about I get back there with you, darlin'. Gonna get cold speeding along." Looking to the driver and grinning. "And got an idea how to keep you warm, same time how you can work off the cost of the fuel and share in the ride. That sound right, Ed?"

"And I guess you expect me to just drive, huh, Arlo?" the driver said to him, grinning through awful teeth.

"Down the road, maybe you can spell me," Arlo said.

Sounded good to Ed. Said he had something he could show this girl alright.

Stella smiled. "Guess you boys can try it, keep me warm and help me go from girl to woman. And guess I got something to show you too . . ." she said, unconcerned, her hand going in her coat pocket, showing the pistol.

"Well now, hold on a minute, we got guns too, missy." Narrowing his eyes, Arlo reached for the rifle.

"Big difference between holding and reaching," she said, cocking it, aiming for his exposed belly, her hand steady now.

"You want to be like that, how about you go on and walk then?"

"How about you dummies get out and do the walking? And you go on and touch it," she said to Ed behind the wheel, "only gonna be one dummy left."

Looking like he was going to jump at her, Arlo said, "Girl, I'm gonna strip you bare-ass and show you—"

And she turned her aim and fired, putting a dime-sized hole in the rear quarter panel, going right through the first barrel, liquid splashing out. Then turning her aim back to the belly, saying to him, "You got any more doubts about it, then go on. But, mister, believe it or not, anything you pull out, I'm gonna shoot it right off." Wagging the pistol, telling the one called Ed to leave it running and hop on out. Waiting until they were both standing at the passenger side.

"Can't get both of us," Arlo said.

"Maybe, but which one?"

The two glanced at each other, Ed half-raising his hands.

"Now, how about you dummies strip down?"

"What's this now?" Arlo said.

"You're gonna show me this something that's going to turn me girl to woman. I'm just curious, that's all. And better not disappoint me either." She could smell the moonshine splashing from the hole she shot in the barrel.

"Changed my mind," Arlo said, folding his arms.

Ed started stripping, believing her.

Firing another round at the ground, she watched Arlo hurrying out of his boots, the two of them tugging off their dirty clothes. Allowing them their long johns and socks full of holes, she had them step out into the field.

"Them barrels is our livelihood, all we got," Arlo called.

"Ought to serve as a lesson then, picking on defenseless girls." Tossing the clothes in back, then getting in, she drove off, passing Auburn and Shenandoah, making it to within five miles from the cropper's shack near Walnut, the old Dodge conking out, its fuel tank dry as the land. Leaving it with its barrels at the side of the road, she walked the rest of the way, the leather of her new shoes pinching her feet.

☾

A Chevy Master sedan sat in the tall grass behind the place. And she found him on the dirty floor of the shack, the front door left open. First thought, he was dying, seeing the blood on his clothes.

Waking, he grinned up at her, "Lost count how many shots they took, a goddamn noise you wouldn't believe. Best they could do is nick me." Touching a finger to his forehead, a couple of scars looking bloody and angry.

"How about you lie still and be quiet." Kneeling next to him, looking where the bullets grazed his forehead, almost in an X. She shuddered, shaking from her mind how close he'd come, checking inside his jacket, making sure he wasn't hit anywhere else.

"Just rattled my cage a bit."

And she pulled him to her, told him to be still. Could tell he was running a fever.

"Not sure how I got here, but looks like I picked up a new car along the way, the bank money's in back. Chevy this time, ain't it? Guess it explains the fever. Looks like I spent the night on the floor, first time I done it without being drunk." Too weak to laugh.

"Shut up, Johnny." Hugging and rocking him, just glad he was alive.

"How'd you make it?"

"Walked out of there, slept under a bridge. Had a couple of fellas give me a lift."

"Good to know, decent folks out there, willing to help."

"Yeah, real good."

"Any idea how many shots they took?"

"You think I stood there counting?"

"Try and guess how many rounds the rangers poured into Bonnie and Clyde's Ford on that Parish road?" He waited, eyes to the ceiling, saying, "Was more'n a hundred and thirty rounds. Maybe they robbed more banks than us, but we're still here talking about it. Think the papers ought to start calling me Unkillable Johnny, instead of Bad Bennie."

Unbuttoning his jacket, she told him to try on Big Mouth Bennie, forcing herself not to cry.

"Ought to take my penitentiary numbers to one of them psychics, you know, see what they mean." Reciting the numbers 39211. "And run them in one of those lotteries they got down in Puerto Rico. You hear of them?"

She told him no, and lay on the floor next to him, and she cradled his head, looking around the place, no running water, nothing she could use to clean the gashes. A couple of holes in his jacket and the scarf she bought him. She found the groove a bullet tore along his shoulder, an angry slash across his flesh. "Well, hate to tell you, mister, your jacket's a wreck for sure, and the shirt too, Egyptian cotton. You know what I paid for it?"

"Lost my hat too."

Stella looked around and didn't see it, saying she'd get him a new one.

"The suitcase? Had that velvet pillow cover I got you in Detroit."

"Afraid they got the case." Stroking his head, wetting the corner of her blouse with her spit, dabbing at his forehead, doing it gentle. "Never cared much about it, no offense."

"Had my Nietzsche in there. *Between Good and Evil*. A nice translation."

"More worried about the lost money than your books."

"Well, if I'm gonna be laid up, I ought to keep up my reading."

"Well, you're nothing but scratched. I'll get you cleaned up, let you heal a bit, then you can go dig up some of the money, go and buy yourself some books. How about that?"

"How about you go out and bring in the sack, keep it close."

Stella went out, having to drag the sewn-together flour sacks filled with the Brookings money.

"Well, at least that went right," he said from the floor, then, "You know, New Orleans is sounding pretty good about now. What say to it?"

"Yeah, I sure could go for one of those po' boys."

"Well, that's what we're doing then. Nobody hunting for us down there. And a hell of a place with its Mardi Gras, Fat Tuesday, and everybody chowing on crawdads and gumbo.

Food as good as it gets, and that jazz music coming from every door. That'll be something, huh?" He winced. "Soon as I'm fit to drive."

"You mean it?"

"This war on Bad Bennie'll wear thin. Who knows, maybe we'll live down there for a while, then maybe go settle back in California. Come back up now and then and see the folks. Get my focus back on my studies while you keep house."

"Keep house, huh? You forgetting about my singing and acting?"

He winked at her, and she helped him sit up, Bennie wanting to go to the door, pointing to the Chevy Master sedan he stole. Bennie saying how he ditched the Buick at this gas station when he stopped for a Coca-Cola. Just left it around the side, then hitchhiked with a trucker, took Bennie to the outskirts of South Clinton. "Where I picked up this beauty, couldn't resist the V8. Hey, why you crying?"

"Got something in my eye, is all." Wiping her eyes with the back of her hand, telling him to go back and lie down, wondering what she could find them to eat.

. . . twenty-two

NOVEMBER 26, 1938

T he director still had that bug up his ass over the Karpis arrest, that crack about Windsor knots.

But things could change in a beat, Werner studying the reports and keeping an eye on the dailies. Thinking as he read, too many of these newspapermen were pressing their lips to Hoover's backside, putting ink down the way he wanted and spinning the truth. Painting Bennie Dickson as a vicious killer. Calling the scene at the Ace Motor Court a gun battle, making it sound like Dickson had been shooting back. Forty-eight rounds fired point blank, the highway patrolmen hitting nothing but barn boards, a few rounds striking Dickson's car. The lawmen acted on a tip and staked out the Ace grounds and had the Dicksons both cold. But the fools left their patrol cars up the block and out of sight and crept up and surrounded the cabin they were in. As Bennie Dickson stepped out in the mid-afternoon sun, the officer in charge called a warning, and Dickson jumped off the steps and ran for the garage — the patrolmen firing like drunk farmers — and Dickson smashed his car out the back, getting away without returning a single shot, blew right past the abandoned patrol cars a block away.

Officers so bent on getting Ben Dickson, they forgot about Stella Mae, the girl walking out the door and slipping behind them while they blasted the garage to kindling. Instead of printing the facts, the papers called it a gun battle. The patrolmen coming away with just a suitcase of souvenirs, a little money and some letters and spare ammo, the agents seizing it and calling it evidence vital to the FBI's case. The same patrolmen later turned up the shot-up Plymouth, handing over more evidence, the agents having it dusted for prints and checked for ballistics.

Werner Hanni shook his head, reading over a report, the first troopers on the scene thought they were coming to question Dickson about the fistfight he got into with clerk Edward Heidt, son of a prominent citizen, at the Topeka motor vehicle office. No idea how it turned into a shooting incident, something that might sum up to an assault charge, at best landing Dickson back in The Walls for a six-month stretch.

Making matters worse, Shawnee County deputies arrested Stella Mae's childhood friend Liz Musick for being mixed up with the Dickson gang. Her family's lawyer springing the innocent girl, guilty only of attending school and roller skating on weekends with Stella Mae over a year ago, having gone to a club with the outlaw couple the night before the so-called gun battle. Looking over the incident reports, Werner Hanni said to nobody, "Whatever else you are, Bennie Dickson, so far, you're fast-thinking or just dumb lucky." Remembering the guy with the bag of laundry back in Brookings, the guy he was looking for standing right next to him, something he'd keep to himself. Reading how young Bennie and his brother Spencer, back when they were Boy Scouts, had saved a local woman from a drowning suicide in a local pond. Not the stuff of public enemies.

Picking up the *Topeka State Journal*, he read about a couple of cars the police seized in repair shops, one a total wreck, another in for repainting, both suspected of belonging to Ben Dickson. Reading another piece how the Redenbaugh family insisted Bennie was a true gentleman, the family unaware he'd served time for car theft and robbing banks. The kind of profile that would have Hoover punching his desk and throwing his phone across the office, something he was rumored to do.

That's when his phone rang, the director himself on the line, wanting to know if Hanni had read the papers, about the time-lock bandits getting away.

"Yes, sir. I've been staying up on it."

"Any idea how much they got away with this time?"

"I believe it was seventeen thousand, sir."

"Seventeen thousand, five hundred and ninety-three dollars. That's just the currency, Hamm. They left with as much in stocks."

"Yes, sir." Werner Hanni held the receiver from his ear. Could hear Hoover crunching up the news release, then yelling into the phone, "Where'd the highway patrol learn to shoot, the county fair?"

"Can't say, sir. Can say the Kansas City office identified the couple, Bennie and Stella Mae Dickson and tracked them to a family farm near Topeka."

"And then lost them."

"Well, they did slip away, but I believe we're closing in, sir." Wanting to remind the director his office wasn't in charge of the case, but knowing if he did he'd get the all-for-one speech again.

"Bank manager said they were polite, quoted right here in ink. Pointed guns in the man's face. How's that polite, Hamm?"

"Of course you're right, sir, but I think—"

"I cannot abide seeing something like that on the front page. Making my phone fly off the ringer. And this Dickson girl's nothing more than a child. Must be dim, is she?"

"Can't say, sir."

"She not hear what fate fell on that Bonnie Parker? Didn't matter she was a girl. You pull a gun and rob a bank, that fairer sex thing they hide behind won't fly. Let it serve a lesson, Hamm. Cross the FBI, and you get crossed right off. Doesn't matter you're a girl."

"Yes, sir."

"And this Dickson, what's your feeling?"

"Ben Dickson, well, sir—"

"He robs the cradle, pervert that he is, puts a gun in her child's hand, and the two of them go robbing banks like a day in the park. Meantime the FBI look like mutts chasing after them, and can't stop them."

"Like I said, sir, I believe we're closing in." Hanni wanting to add that was the sentiment of Ed Guinane, the SAC at the Kansas City office. Nothing to do with Werner Hanni and the Aberdeen office, suspecting this was more about Hoover getting back at Hanni for the necktie thing.

"Except they lost them, let them slip right through."

"That was the locals, sir. But it's just a matter of—"

"A Bonnie and Clyde revival, eluding the G-man is what they're saying around the capitol, saying it behind my back. Making a meal out of it with their poisoned ink." The director sighed into the phone, then, "Ought to try wearing my pants sometime, Hamm. See what it feels like."

"No, sir. I mean, I understand your position, sir, but I should mention—"

"Stop dancing around, Hamm. Just spit it out."

"Well, since linking the two banks and IDing the suspects, Kansas City's staked out the family places and the garages where the two cars were—"

"I been talking for five minutes, and you don't lead with something like that? Must think I got nothing to do but play golf with Assistant Director Tolson, or go watch the ponies. What else are you not saying, Hamm?"

"Been looking over Benjamin Dickson's sheet. Says he's served time for bank robbery and car theft."

"So, you're telling me . . . what are you telling me?"

"Special agent in charge of the case, Ed Guinane, thinks Dickson stole the Buick outside of Kansas City, the black convertible used in the second bank job."

"And this Dickson gets a teenaged girl mixed up in it."

"His wife, sir. Stella Mae, sixteen years old. Lived with her folks in—"

"Going to hell in a bucket, Hamm, we got teenagers robbing banks, and getting away in a stolen convertible."

"Yes, sir. I got kids my—"

"Report says they forced the bankers at gunpoint, took 'em hostage and fled across state lines."

"Dickson stood the bankers on the running boards like shields and drove a couple blocks, let them off by the court-house. The bankers crossed to the Beatrice Creamery, made the call to the locals. And they put out an all-points and set up roadblocks."

"Time lock in the bank, the robbers sitting around waiting on the vault to pop, and not a lawman in sight. Says they got an eyewitness swears the Buick just rolled out of town with bankers on the running boards like a parade float with nobody noticing them waltz right out of town. And long gone by the time the locals thought about setting up their roadblock."

"That's the way I understand it, sir."

"Got another report from a kid at the White Eagle Filling Station, corner of Sixth and Medary. Claims the girl scattered a box of roofing nails out her window and on to the road, guess to hinder the lawmen."

"Yes, sir."

"Lawmen outwitted by a teenage girl. All our resources and technology, and she's armed with roofing nails. I want them stopped, Hamm, stopped hard."

"Are you saying—"

"'Course we can't go around shooting teenage girls. Just think of the ink — God, man. We'd have a martyred saint on our hands, a kid with pimples. It's this Dickson we want. The man robs the cradle, then robs the bank. Hey, that's not bad."

Hanni still wanting to slip in how the case was in the hands of Ed Guinane and the Kansas City office, but knowing it would get him Hoover's we're-a-team speech, or worse, it could end with him on a bus to Anchorage.

"What else you got, Hamm?"

"Well, from talking with Ed Guinane, I learned the couple spent a night at a family farm near Tyler. He suspects they're still in the area and lying low."

"That where you lost them, this place called Tyler?"

"If you like, sir, I can call Agent Guinane, ask him to report directly to you. But I'm sure he'll tell you the same thing, how it's just a matter of—"

"Sick of hearing you say it, Hamm. You know what it gets me thinking?"

"I got an idea, sir."

"The temperature in Alaska, any idea?"

"I'm betting on cold, sir."

"That's just a matter of time too." And the line went dead.

. . . twenty-three

NOVEMBER 27, 1938

Stella was thinking he actually believed what he was saying, telling her how they'd go hide in New Orleans, even mentioned going to Mexico, learn the lingo and get nice and tanned, feeding on shrimp and beans. Promising her someplace safe, where they weren't being hunted. But then he just drove her all over the Plains, dodging lawmen like it was a game, hiding stolen money at his railcar and out back of his family's farm. Abandoning the cropper's shack, he drove them somewhere near Beatrice, and here they were, pitching camp, middle of no place.

Didn't matter what he said, she had this feeling like the law was closing in. Stella had seen their photos and names on the wanted dodger at the Walnut postal office, Bennie looking dangerous in the front and profile views, the mugshot showing his Missouri State Pen numbers and the FBI number: 395908. His age and description. The one of her was an old class photo. Taken before that man took her from the roller rink and did those things and wrecked her life. Stella couldn't believe the words: Most Wanted. Knowing the lawmen had taken it from her mother's family album.

Kneeling with his back to her, his shirt off, Bennie pounded the tent pegs, the spot with a good vantage point, could see the back road below them. The Buick parked next to them.

"Now, it's Mexico, huh?" Stella could see the distant dust rising, looked like a car was coming this way. Could smell the must coming off the folded canvas of the tent he was pitching, expecting her to sleep in it, promising it would just be a night or two.

"Well, it's just one idea. They got Tijuana and Ensenada, real party towns. Got this drink with a worm in it."

"Think I'd like that, huh, worm in my drink?"

"We just stay there till they forget about us. We'll come back for our money and go settle in California. Can finish my studies and buy that house we talked about." Bennie setting up the pup tent, army green and barely big enough for the two of them to squeeze into.

He kept the pain in his head to himself, not wanting her to worry, knowing she'd want him to go see a doctor. Saying, "We could start a business, a shop you can run."

"Now you want me to be a shopkeeper?"

"Well, just till I finish school, can sell knicknacks, souvenirs, sandwiches if you want, something like that. Of course, as a lawyer's wife, you wouldn't need to do any of that."

"Johnny."

"And no more Johnny. Just going to settle down and be Ben Dickson, the used-to-be bank robber and prize fighter turned citizen. Who knows, maybe I'll write a book when the statute runs out. Tell about robbing banks and dodging the law. They ask why I did it, I'll say on account that's the only place the money was. Talk about how I put myself through law school." Laughing and shaking his head. "A crook goes to law school, could be the title."

"Johnny!" Stella saw the dust rising past the trees down-slope. Whoever was driving was coming fast.

"Come away with a better grasp of what the ones I'm representing went through." Hammering at the last tent peg, he struck a rock, having to pull the peg back, stretching the rope and driving it in again.

"Johnny!" She was looking past the trees.

The tone of her voice had him rising and looking behind him. Then they could hear the engines, more than one, and saw the glint of chrome. Catching her by the wrist, saying, "Remember what I told you. Now go."

And she turned and ran across the clearing for the woods.

Getting in the car and cranking the engine, he watched her going for the trees, calling, "You run like a girl." Waiting and watching the two cars pull up below, stopping side by side, blocking the road. Taking the rifle from behind the seat, he watched the four men getting behind the open car doors, Bennie turned to see Stella make it into the trees, then she was out of sight.

"Bennie Dickson, throw down your weapons. You're under arrest."

"Funny you'd see it that way," he said to himself and fired a couple of rounds, working the bolt, keeping the lawmen pinned behind their doors. It only allowed them to bob up and snap quick shots, most of them going wide, Bennie hearing one bullet strike the back end of the Buick. Guessing Stella was through the trees and out the other side, he left the tent and supplies, got in and drove from the camp spot, angling downhill, hoping he had it right, the back way out of there.

. . . twenty-four

NOVEMBER 28, 1938

"Papers say they fired forty-eight rounds at the Ace Motor Court, said maybe I got mortally wounded. Liars. Goddamn barely nicked me."

"Yeah, yeah, you told me, about a hundred times now." Stella rolling her eyes, getting bored with it.

"Never kept count, but must have fired a dozen or more shots back at the campground."

"You gonna call yourself unkillable again, think I'm gonna throw up."

"Just making conversation." Since picking her up at the roadside, the other side of the hill from the campground, he couldn't drive ten miles on account of the dizziness. He told her to take the wheel, saying he was sick of doing all the driving anyway. Something she should learn how to do, pull her weight around here.

Never driven at night, she leaned with her nose close to the steering wheel, trying to see ahead on the dark road.

Saying the headlights were aimed wrong. And that sound coming from under the hood had her worried too.

"Well, cars do that, make all rattling kinds of sounds to keep you guessing. Makes you feel better, we'll get her to a mechanic when we get to Detroit. Let them look under the hood. That or we just steal a new one." Bennie thinking this wreck wouldn't make it halfway. Not sure what was wrong, but it sounded bad. Guessing you could only shoot up a V8 so much before it gave out.

"And you best get somebody to look at you too."

"There you go, worrying your head again. I told you I'm fine. Think I'd know, right? On top of I can't just walk in some doctor's office. Everybody seen my picture in every paper and post office wall. The kind of thing they're expecting."

"Stick on your glasses and one of your aliases, tell them you're a traveler, going to the coast like everybody else. Tell them you had a misfortune and took a knock to the head."

"It's just a headache, it'll pass. And for right now, that's the last of my worries. We get to the next town, I'll walk in some drugstore, see about getting some pills or something. That suit you, lady?"

"You going in places, flashing all that money—"

"There you go, off on something else. You don't want me burying it, you don't want me carrying it. What's left, let's go shopping? Jesus!"

"It's just a lot of walking-around money, and no, I don't want you burying it. And where you gonna shop, one of your campgrounds?" Frowning, realizing she was angry, Bennie having her drive north instead of south, believing it would throw the law off their trail.

"Don't know what you want?"

"How about we just tuck some under the spare tire."

"And how about if we ditch the car quick?"

"Alright, forget it, Johnny." She banged her palms against the wheel.

They were quiet, a couple miles of listening to the gravel road under them, along with the ailing engine.

"Back to calling me Johnny, huh?" He smiled, trying to bring her back.

"And you're back to ducking my questions."

"Not even sure what it was."

"Said to forget it." Stella looked at a crossroad ahead, asking which way to go, these back roads unmarked. Guessing they were coming up on Kalamazoo, a signpost some miles back said they were on State Highway 60.

He pointed right, saying, "Okay, I'll see some doctor. But on hiding more money, think if we got to make another run, like at the Ace place, we'll be glad it's on us. Instead of them getting it."

"Maybe there's no good place."

"You go long enough without any, it feels pretty good having it close." He patted the roll in his pocket. Looking out, he saw another fork coming, told her to go straight, then, "Maybe it reminds me like I'm getting someplace."

"*You're* getting, huh?"

"Of course I mean you and me. It's always you and me, you know that."

"With our money squirreled over half of Kansas." Giving him a weak smile.

"There you go, sounding like my girl. Now, how long I gotta go thirsty?" He leaned close for a kiss, feeling dizzy and nauseous, trying not to let it show. "But maybe you got a point, you ought to be right there, see where I stash it, just in case, uh, we get split up or something. Gonna draw it up like a treasure map, the two places we already got, next pencil I see."

"A treasure map, huh?"

"Yeah. Just got to do it so nobody else can make heads or tails of it."

"You were gonna say get shot."

"What?"

"You said split up, but you were gonna say get shot."

"Well . . . you're one smart cookie, you know it, lady? And me, guess I'm just plain lucky to have you along."

"Turning the talk around again, the way you do." Pointing a finger at him.

"Had forty-eight shots fired at me, and I barely got a scratch, and I'm still good looking."

Stella thinking how the G-men put Dillinger down, coming out of that theater with *Manhattan Melodrama* playing. Shot him in back of his neck. And Clyde Barrow driving into a rain of bullets.

"You thinking it just takes one, a bullet," he said.

"You reading my mind now?"

"Can tell the way you clamp your jaw, like you're wanting to say something, but holding yourself back from it."

"Was thinking something, how Dillinger and the Barrows ended up."

"Well, I'd rather be like Willie Sutton. Man gets caught and uses his noodle to bust out again and again. Never been shot. Yeah, best to be like that."

"Sounds like your head's getting big as well as scratched up."

"Hey now, how about that water?" Bennie with a burning thirst, felt like no matter how much he drank he was still thirsty, guessing he was running a fever. Been that way since the Ace Motor Court. Hoping they found some abandoned place they could rest soon. Then he saw the lights up ahead.

"Yeah, only water we got's in the radiator. That is, if you don't mind it hot." She knew he was burning with fever. Seeing the lights up ahead, two cars along the ditch, looked like a breakdown.

"Likely a son of the soil, with a load of cucumbers or something, late getting them to market and busted down," Bennie said, knowing nothing was growing in these badlands, not since the drought that took hold nearly a decade back. Reaching the back of the convertible for his hat, putting it on and pulling it low.

Stella saying, "Don't think they got cucumbers, Johnny." A Ford with the hood on its prop rod, a state trooper's car behind it. Two uniformed men standing there, watching as they approached. No way to avoid driving past them, not without drawing more attention.

Checking over the stalled car, the troopers looked over as they passed. The Buick sounding like it was set to conk out.

"Just eye the road, and take it easy." Bennie gave a wave to the officers, trying to hide his face.

"Told you we should be going south," she said.

"We get to Detroit, we'll route back down." Bennie checked his mirror, saying, "Maybe change our looks. Me with a mustache. Maybe you crop and color your hair."

"What's wrong with the color of my hair?" She touched a hand to it, never thought of changing it before. "Mother calls it my best feature." Glancing back at the road behind her, the two troopers still standing and looking after them.

"Well, yeah, sure it's a good one. You're just ripe with best features. Idea's not to get spotted, that's all. And any color hair's fine by me. Red maybe."

"Red, huh?"

"Maybe just for a while." Bennie glanced over his shoulder, smiled at her. "Be fun trying it out, huh?" Running a finger above his lip like a mustache.

"Fun for who?"

But he didn't answer, just said, "How you think I'd look, a little one like Cesar Romero, you see him in *Diamond Jim*?"

"You think you look like him, huh?"

"I don't know. Who you think I look like? Maybe a young William Powell."

"Was thinking more like Oliver Hardy."

"Think you got a mean streak, lady." Bennie glanced over the backseat, the troopers gone from view now. "Just grow it out, then if I don't like it, or you say it tickles, I'll shave it off. And hey, what say you step on it some there, granny?"

"Think they seen us? Got our wanted dodgers all over the place."

"Naw, too dark for it, but those boys might've spotted the out-of-state plate, heard the knocking engine, maybe got their attention. But don't worry your head about it. They're not coming, but step on it anyway."

"Nearly got my foot to the boards. You not hear it, that grinding. Something's not right."

"Take the next side road, we'll find a spot with cover and wait till morning. Give me a chance for a look under the hood."

"Got a bad feeling about them back there, the way they were looking. Just want to get as far as we can."

"A country this size, not enough lawmen to cover every inch, and those two were busy with the wreck. They can't be in all the places where a man can hide, and no point killing the car."

"The law seems to want to kill *us* pretty bad."

"The next bank robber comes along and gets their attention, they're gonna give 'em something new, and they'll forget all about the Dicksons." Bennie sounding like he was getting tired of her worrying.

"Wish I was as sure as you."

"Hell, it's only been two banks. Old Dillinger hit so many he made off with over a million bucks. You imagine money like that, a million bucks? Why he's known as the dean, or the jackrabbit, because they just couldn't catch up to him."

"Except when they shot him." Stella bored with hearing about Dillinger.

"Still public enemy number one in my book."

"Dead's dead, Bennie." She turned on the seat, not wanting to say that he didn't always have to say something smart, like he liked the sound of his own voice. That's when she saw the lights coming behind her.

And he saw them too.

"Think those cops are sharper than you think." She stomped at the pedal, not getting much for it.

"Shit! Come on, girl, pump it."

"What d'you think I'm doing?"

The howler started behind them. The lights flashing as the patrol car gained.

"Told you something's wrong." Stella banged her foot on the pedal.

"Here, switch with me." Bennie not waiting, tugging her arm and pulling her roughly across, setting her on the passenger side. Slapping the steering wheel like it was a nag, he veered the Buick and kept them from the ditch. "Come on, baby, show me something." He tromped the pedal. Thinking he should have laid the shotgun on the floor behind the seat, not in the trunk. The patrol car gaining fast.

Swerving wide onto the next farm road, he got the back end sliding on the loose dirt, raising dust, the engine clanging, a grinding howl starting from under the hood. The two cars nearly bumper to bumper now. Bennie made another hard right turn, and the patrol car shot past them, grinding, screeching and swerving to a stop. Switching off his lights, Bennie corrected the steering when he felt the soft shoulder. Kept them moving. The next farm track came up fast, and he turned left onto it, the car's tires rocking in the ruts, the chassis bumping over rough ground, being guided by the ruts like a railcar. Crashing through some scrub, he turned behind a patch of trees, bottoming out hard, getting the car out of sight, shutting off the engine. Waiting till the patrol car whipped past on the farm track, raising dust in the night.

A minute passed and he got out, hearing the sound of the cop car fading. He stumbled to the road, fighting the dizziness, watching and listening. Looking to see that Stella couldn't see him, he dropped to his knees and he threw up, hoping she couldn't hear him do it. Feeling the damp on his forehead, just the night sounds of mockingbirds. Wiping his face, he was thinking another Buick let him down, then he shrugged, letting it off; it had been shot too.

Too dark to pull up the hood and have a look, he got back in, got it started and backed out to the road. Figuring the cops would be coming back figuring out his move, he drove with no lights, backtracking their way to the two-lane. The engine hacking and grinding.

Backtracked a couple of miles before he saw the lights coming up behind them again and gaining, closing the distance.

"Shit."

No howler or flashing lights this time, the cop on the passenger side had his hat off and was hanging out the window, and he started unloading pistol shots, firing into the Buick. Swerving back and forth, Bennie hoped to raise enough dust, not giving them a clear target, yelling for Stella to get down. The goddamn shotgun in the trunk. Should've got it when he stopped by the trees.

Leaning down, Stella fished the .38 from under the seat, turned herself around on the seat, reached and unzipped the convertible's back window.

Bennie yelling at her to get down.

"Just watch the road." Barking back at him, propping against the dash, her feet on the seat, getting leverage against the dashboard, clicking off the safety, she cocked and aimed.

The cop on the passenger side kept firing, bullets thudding into the rear end.

"Last time I'm telling you—" Yelling, he wanted to yank her down.

Her head was knocked back into the windshield. She cried out, blood streaming from the side of her head, dripping on her clothes, onto the floor.

Calling her name, Bennie clutched for her, kept fishing back and forth, slowing down, nothing to do but give up.

"Sons of bitches." Touching a hand to her head, seeing the blood. Shaking Bennie off, she raised up, saying, "You hold this heap steady." Getting up against the dash, planting her feet again, she leaned across the open back, aiming and firing twice.

A sharp screech and the headlights of the patrol car vanished to her left. They heard the crashing as the patrol car rolled down the ditch, the two cops tossed inside. The patrol car tearing through a mangled section of fence, tumbling over and back onto its wheels, the roof crushed down.

Bennie stopped in the road and looked at her, blood showing in her hair. Stella gave him a weak smile, putting together what happened, then seeing blood on his jacket, believing he'd been shot, and she grabbed at him.

"It's not me, it's you." Bennie holding her at arm's length, looking at her, her face a mask of dark and wet. Pulling her close, looking for a wound, he checked her eyes, then looked back at the road. Just wanted to get out, take the shotgun or rifle from the trunk and go and finish those two men, hoping the crash had done it for him.

))

"Where'd you learn to shoot like that, lady?" Coaxing the Buick ten more miles, he stopped along a line of shelter belt trees planted in a long row to make a windbreak between the barren fields, the poplars keeping the winds from stirring the dirt into the dust clouds from hell that had plagued the Midwest for years. Bennie feeling dizzy, his vision blurred.

Too dark to get a real good look at Stella's wound, so he dabbed a kerchief, wetting a corner and wiping away at the blood, some of it in her hair, told her it just nicked her and wasn't so bad, but guessing there could be a scar. "I tell you, that was some shooting," he said again. "You see the way they flew off the road. I thought we were done."

"I had a pretty fair teacher, started me out with tin cans."

"Went from tin cans to tin badges."

"Guess I surprised them, a woman shooting back . . ." She told him she was fine and pushed his hand away. "You're just getting spit all over me. Said I'm fine, except maybe I'll have a scar like you. That bother you?"

"Just some honest damage; you're still the prettiest girl around." Raising his finger. "But I did tell you to get down."

Stella bit at the finger, saying, "If I listened, where'd we be now?"

161

Pulling back the finger, he said, "Makes you feel better, imagine the scars and damage on them two, flipping down that ditch. Teach them about shooting at the fairer sex. And I got to admit, if you hadn't done it, those fellows'd be rolling our fingers in ink by now, and locking up the cell door."

"Just a couple lucky shots. I was going for the headlight. Lucky I hit anything with all that shaking."

"Ought to put you in one of those fairs. Could be the next Annie Oakley. Get you doing some trick shooting while I drive you around a circus ring like a wild man with a V8." Bennie smiled, his head throbbing, his stomach rolling.

"Instead we best keep to the shadows."

"Right. And first thing, we need fresh wheels, this one's done. We head east, Indiana, then Michigan. Lay low, then we back-road it down to the gulf, then on to the coast if we feel like it. Go at night mostly. Nobody looking for us down there."

Praying the car would make it to Springfield, Bennie thinking they'd have to come back to dig up more money another time, knowing they'd need it, likely have to keep away from this part of the country longer than he told her.

... *twenty-five*

NOVEMBER 29, 1938

The middle of no place, three in the morning. Bennie pushed himself and the car, betting the cops put out an all-points bulletin, trying to put them in a box. From the sound of what was coming from under the hood, they wouldn't make another five miles, and Stella's head was bleeding again. Bennie fighting the spins, the nausea, feeling the burn of the fever.

"Any idea where we are?" Touching a finger to her gash, feeling the wet blood. Looking at him in the dark, guessing he was hiding how he was feeling, hadn't been right since the cops shot up that garage.

"Some place around Vicksburg." Putting them twenty miles south of Kalamazoo, Bennie making out the silhouette of a farmhouse roof, pulling past its mailbox and into its yard, the place dark. Leaving the engine running, he told her to stay in the car, adding, "I mean it this time." Leaving his door hanging open in case the farmer had a dog, Bennie not wanting to shoot a dog for doing its job. Buttoning his jacket, he went up the porch steps, knocked and waited, glad he didn't hear any barking. Rapping harder and waiting.

No lights came on, but he heard creaking inside. An old man pulled back the door, asked what he wanted.

"I'm out of gas. Hoping you can help us out."

The old man told him to wait there, left the door open and said he was going to get his son. The younger man coming to the door was about thirty, a slight build and a tangle of hair.

Bennie was back to calling himself Johnny O'Malley. "Hope you can help us out, me and the missus."

"Guess I can try." Said he was Claude Minnis, then, "What's the trouble?"

"Ran out of gas."

"But she's running." Claude nodded at the car.

"Mean we're down to the drops, and she's not sounding right. Afraid to turn her off."

Looking at him in the dim light, Claude thought a moment, saying, "Not sure I can help."

"How about if I insist?" Bennie pulled the Colt from inside his jacket. "Afraid I got to ask for your car."

"What kind of trouble you in, mister?" Claude said, seeing the gashes crisscrossing Bennie's forehead, looking into the Buick, seeing Stella on the passenger side. "You're them two, ain't you? Bank-robbing couple everybody's looking for. Yeah, sure, recognize you from the Most Wanted at the general."

"I asked where's your car."

"Call you the Dickson Gang, making you Bad Bennie."

"You don't want to know how bad I can get. Now, the car, how about we have a look?" Bennie motioned with the pistol, getting Claude to lead the way down the steps and out to the barn.

An old Chevy truck sat inside, Claude pulling the complaining door back and climbing onto the seat, working to start it, but unable to get it to catch, shaking his head. "Got a mule if you want."

Bennie told him to get out, climbing in and trying it himself, saying he was surely car-cursed. Everything going the wrong way. "You got a telephone here?"

"Nope." Claude shook his head, saying, "Closest one'd be town, the general store. Charges fifty cents to use it, if you can believe that. You wanna talk about robbery."

"What's the closest place around, like a neighbor?"

Claude pointed past the shadow of a tree to the north, the top of a silo showing past it, saying the Metis place was a half mile, said old man Metis didn't have a phone either.

Bennie telling him to get in, waving him around the passenger side of the Buick.

"Can't leave my pop on account he's near blind."

"You call in the house, say you got to tend the mule, be back soon."

Bennie watched him go to the door and call inside, coming back down the steps and getting in the ailing Buick. Stella sliding across, sitting between them with her .38 in her lap. Claude introducing himself, said he was pleased to meet her, seeing the dried blood.

Egging the Buick to make it, Bennie asked, "So, who's this fellow lives there?"

"Henry Metis."

"He got a dog?"

"Thought you were after his car?"

Bennie looked at him.

Claude saying, "No, he ain't got no dog. None I know of."

Bennie pulled into the farmstead as the engine cut out. He was looking at a modest place with an upstairs, no light showing from inside. The shadows of a barn and the silo behind it.

Opening the passenger door, Claude stepped up on the running board and hollered for Henry.

After a minute a light came on upstairs, and after another minute the front door opened. A big man stood in his nightshirt, wanting to know what was going on, looking at Claude with the strangers.

Claude telling Bennie this was Henry Metis.

"I know who I am," Henry said. "Who you got with you, Claude? You been drinking—"

Showing the pistol, Bennie went up the steps and said, "Nice to meet you, Henry. Afraid I'll have to cut right to it. What I'm after's your car." He held on to the porch post.

"The hell you say?" Henry just looked at him, one hand at his hip, the other still holding the door.

"Need to borrow it a while."

"You can't come take a man's car, middle of the night."

"Well, Sam Colt says different." Showing it to him.

Standing there, Henry thought a moment, the November cold not bothering him. Saying, "Well, goddamn it." Trying to rush at Bennie, catching his sleeve on the doorknob, Henry shook free of it and swung an all-day haymaker.

Claude jumped out of the way.

In spite of the fever, it was an easy duck under the swing. Bennie said, "Now, come on and stop this, fella." Telling Stella to get back in the car. Stella reaching under the seat for the .38.

Henry wound and swung again, grunting and putting a slow weight behind the turn of his hip, punching the porch post that time, a heavy thud shaking the whole porch. Crying out, grabbing his sore knuckles in his other hand, calling Bennie a son of a bitch.

"Come on now, Henry, you need those farming hands, you got work to do." Bennie got out of the way of the next one, a clumsy uppercut. The meaty fist with no speed swishing past him, Henry having to regain his balance.

Coming off the porch, Bennie gave himself some room, his Colt down at his side, saying, "You about done, Henry?"

"I look done to you?" And the big man went after him again, his bare feet on the rough ground, trying with his left, grunting and swinging for Bennie's head. Didn't matter about the pistol in the smaller man's hand.

In spite of the dizziness, Bennie slipped and ducked and sidestepped a couple more. Feeling sorry for the dirt farmer, letting him punch himself out.

"Slippery son of a bitch, I'll give you that." Henry puffed harder, his punches swished the air, his frosty breath puffing out. Ended with his hands on his knees, bent over and gulping in air. The tops of the right knuckles skinned and bleeding.

"Okay now, we got that worked out." Bennie had a look around and went to the car next to the house. "Nice Ford. What's this, a thirty-five, Henry?"

"Thirty-four." Henry and Claude lagging behind, Stella behind them with her pistol.

"She got the V8?"

"What d'I need that for?" Henry said.

Bennie frowned, saying, "I'm gonna ask you fellas to come along for a ride. Won't keep you too long, and I'm gonna pay you for your time, providing Henry quits swinging at me. How's that sound?"

"You're talking like we got a say," Claude said.

"As far as your car, what say I buy it from you? Be happy to post you the money. And I'm aiming to treat you square on the price, just so we got an understanding."

"A thief treating me square," Henry said.

Claude said to Henry this was Bad Bennie Dickson.

"And you brung 'em round my place?" Henry said to him.

"Didn't have much say in the matter."

"Let me ask," Bennie said, "you fellas keep your money in a bank?"

"No, sir. Keep it in a safe place," Claude said. "Wouldn't trust them sons of bitches, and you can put your gun on me, I'm not going to tell you where I got it."

"Well, I got no argument, and so you know, I'm not after your money. Just getting you to see me man to man."

"Talking like we're on the same side," Henry said. "Hard to speak free when one man's holding a pistol, set on taking my car."

"The whole time you're swinging your fist, I had my gun. Could've done you anytime I wanted."

"Guess that makes us chums then."

Bennie frowned and nodded to the Buick, thinking he might throw up again, saying, "How about you boys just set our gear in the trunk of your car." Pointing the Colt to the back of the Ford. Glancing at Stella, thinking her bleeding stopped. Then back to the two men. "And I'm gonna ask you to ride with us to the Indiana line. Set you loose as soon as we cross."

"Told you my old man's blind," Claude said.

"I got no choice, same as you, but I promise to set you loose soon as we cross."

"And you're gonna keep my car?" Henry said.

"Like I said, I aim to buy her, V8 or not. Everything goes right, you'll be back home by morning. And the money'll be coming. And for what it's worth, the Buick's yours."

"How much money?" Henry wanted to know.

☾

"Didn't tell me about the speed limiter," Bennie said, sitting behind the wheel, Henry next to him helping him with directions, Stella and Claude in back. Frustrated with this heap, Bennie couldn't believe Henry Ford put such a thing in one of his cars, the limiter not allowing the speedometer to climb above forty-five.

"Wife figured it's a good idea. On nights I come home after poker," Henry said, shrugging. "Never thought about it much, all these dirt roads and how fast can a man go anyway?"

"Well, it's something I should've known up front, the type of thing that puts a deal off," Bennie said. "I'll pay you rent for using her, but no way I'm buying her."

"Well now, maybe you got the gun, but I get duped. Wasn't me who got you out of bed, insisting on taking my car."

"That's the same bridge, one we passed fifteen minutes back." Stella said from the backseat, tapping Bennie's shoulder.

Henry forced a grin, looking back at her, saying, "My mistake."

"Seems our Henry's running us in circles, talking about his fair play." Taking the rifle from the rear floor, she threw back the bolt, saying, "Running us in a loop, wanting the cops to catch up." Taking a cartridge, she set it in the breech and pushed the bolt, letting Henry see it.

Shaking his head, Henry looked back at her, saying, "Missy, you ain't gonna—"

The shot tore through the roof, everybody jumping.

Waiting for the ringing in her ears to ease, she said, "I see that bridge again, Henry, your head's gonna look like a dropped pumpkin. You believe it?"

"You don't believe it, then you don't know her like I do," Bennie said to Henry, his head pounding, his ears ringing.

Stella smiled at Claude next to her, putting in another shell, leaning the barrel across the seat, just past Henry's shoulder.

"All the same to you, Henry," Claude said, "I just as soon not go deaf. You direct these folks by here one more time, I'm gonna want to shoot you myself." Looking at Stella, saying, "If that's alright with you, ma'am."

"Let me tell you something, Henry," Bennie said. "Lawmen catch up while you're running us in circles, I promise you it's the car they'll be shooting at, won't be particular who's in it. Won't matter as long as they get us. What they'll do is spin the story for the papers when it's all shot up and done, same way they did to Bonnie and Clyde. Guess you read about it, maybe seen the pictures?"

Henry just pointed ahead, told Bennie to forget what he just said and changed his directions, told him to hook a right a mile up. "Guess it's maybe four, five miles to the state line."

"And we get there, like I said, you fellas are free to go. But you want to cross with us, go a few miles more, well, we're gonna make it worth your while."

"You mean pay us so it don't look like kidnapping across the state line?" Claude wanting to be clear.

"Guess you know about the law."

"You mind making it plainer, what exactly you mean by worth our while?" Henry said.

"Well, the G-man hears about robbing banks and stolen cars, kidnapping and crossing state lines — the way their minds work — they see us as a public menace, giving them grounds to take aim and go to town."

Claude nodded like that made sense, said he read about the shootout at the Ace Motor Court a week back. "Guessing it's why you keep changing cars."

"And how about if my car gets all shot up?" Henry said, looking at the hole in his roof.

"Pay you two dollars a hole, how's that? Look, I don't want any hard feelings, just one man giving another one a hand up, and everybody getting what's coming."

"You take my car, want us keeping mum and facing obstruction charges, all on the layaway plan . . ." Henry said.

"Bennie reached in his pocket for the roll of cash. "Like I said, I'd buy the car except for that limiter and no V8, but I'll pay the rent and for the hole you already got. Plus some more for your troubles." Looking back at Claude, saying, "Throwing in the Buick back at Henry's. You can do what you want with it."

"That car's all shot up."

"Yeah, but it's a Buick. Now, I'll ask you boys how much is fair for your troubles?" Bennie counted out some bills, doing it slow, the bills in his hands on top of the steering wheel.

"I don't know, what do you think, Claude?" Henry said, his eyes not leaving the folding money.

"Guess we ain't been treated so bad . . ." Leaning forward, Claude said to Bennie, "Except for me having to leave my blind old pop. Can picture the fear going through the poor man."

Folding his arms, Henry shook his head, saying he sure hated to leave his car, having to wait in hopes of getting paid. "Sell it to you for what I paid, cash on the spot, but otherwise I can't say we got no deal. 'Less we're back to pointing guns."

Bennie was tired of the big fool, seeing lights coming toward him, another car approaching, relieved to see it wasn't the state troopers.

Henry was waving his arms for help as the Studebaker pulled close.

And Stella touched the rifle to his ear.

"Let him fuss all he wants," Bennie said, swerving the Ford and blocking the other car, a lone man inside stopping. The cars bumper to bumper. Getting out, Bennie went to the driver's door and tapped his pistol against the window, saying, "Need to borrow your car, mister." Then asking the man's name.

Louis Karr said he was on his way to an early meeting, had a customer in Kankakee, looking at the wounds X-ing across Bennie's forehead, then at the pistol in his hand.

Bennie held up a finger, wanting him to wait a moment, turned his head and threw up bile, wiped his mouth, then said, "How much you make in a day, Louis?" Counting out five one-dollar bills, Bennie gave it to him, said it was to make up for lost wages. Then asked about Louis's hat, paying him another five for the porkpie, looking like it would fit loose enough not to hurt while hiding his gashes. Watching Louis Karr putting away his money.

Bennie told Claude to drive Henry's Ford with Louis next to him, Stella in the back.

"Where am I gonna be?" Henry asked like he wasn't happy about it.

Bennie opened the trunk of the Studebaker, telling the big man to get in. "Had enough of you for one day, Henry."

"Got no air in there," Henry complained, refusing to do it.

Finding a length of rope in the trunk, Bennie shoved the big man in, tying the trunk lid so Henry could keep it open enough without suffocating from the exhaust. Behind the wheel of the Studebaker with the Ford following, Bennie drove until they got caught at a railway crossing a dozen miles outside of Valparaiso, waiting on a slow freight. Cursing his luck, Bennie got out and watched Henry escape from the Studebaker's trunk, the man somehow cutting the rope, doing it without Stella seeing him. The man running across the field, waving at the train.

Getting out with the .38 in her hand, Stella said, "You want me to wing him, bring him down?"

"Not worth it." Bennie got Claude and Louis to move their belongings to the back of the Studebaker, leaving them with the Ford, told them to turn around and drive back the way they came. Wishing them a good day, Bennie and Stella got in and waited on the passing freight to go by.

. . . *twenty-six*

DECEMBER 1, 1938

"Pull up some dust," he said, watching her walk up the steps of the rooming house, drafty and dirty. The scar wasn't as angry now, mostly hidden by her hair. He folded up the *Kansas City Journal* and set it on the porch.

"You ever get tired of reading about yourself?"

"Checking the want ads, trying to buy us a fresh car." Looking at her, sizing up her mood, taking his roll of Life Savers, taking the next one, pineapple. There had been an article talking about the thousand news releases the FBI put out. Called Bennie a two-bit boxer turned crook, and claimed her to be wayward. Witness statement by Henry Metis called Bennie a stone-cold killer, telling how he slugged the so-called boxer, outfoxed them both and made his escape across a field while they waited on a passing freight, lucky to get away with his life with them taking potshots at him.

"Know you'd like to spend time with the family, and I guess I miss mine too." Bennie knowing they couldn't go anywhere near that part of the state.

"Well, with Christmas coming it would be nice, but I understand we can't," she said. "Be something to get the folks together, though, both sides, yours and mine."

"Yeah, get you cooking me that home-cooked meal. Turkey and stuffing would do the trick. Not getting out of that one, you know?"

"Well, you want home cooking, maybe when we stop running for our lives." The smile was weak. "'Less you find a car with a kitchen in the jump seat."

"Yeah, you really can cook, huh?" Bennie trying to keep the mood light.

"Mother showed me a thing or two, like any girl. And someday I'll prove it to you, cook anything you want."

"Big bird with all the trimmings, *mmm*, man, that sounds just fine. Good looking and the girl can cook as good as she shoots. Well, just go and call me lucky." Folding up the paper, he stood, stretched his hundred-year-old back and said, "Pretty soon, we'll start sliding from the G-man's memory. Could be plating up supper sooner than you think." Sticking the paper in a back pocket.

"Unless you get nosing around another bank."

"No, lady, we're done with it, I promise you that."

She went to him and put her arms around his neck, eyeing his crisscrossing scars. That terrible feeling not lifting off her lately — like she was going to lose him — holding him tight against her. She told him she was glad to hear it.

"Hey, careful, I'm still a healing man," Bennie said.

And easing her hug, she said, "So, this car you're looking to buy, guess it means we're leaving again."

"Guy in the paper's trying to sell a Ford for forty bucks, but sounds like too good a deal, you know?"

"What happened to being a Buick man?"

"Well, I'm always one at heart, but I'm thinking if the G-man's figured that much, then that's what they'll expect." Bennie winked, said the only thing that really mattered was the V8. Henry Ford's being as good as anybody's.

"You gonna miss seeing your name in the papers, I mean since we quit?"

"Well, guess I got a kick from it, but I know I hurt my folks, yours too, people expecting more from me. And you, I think I let you down the most."

"I always saw a choice in it. Knew what it was I was getting into."

"Guess you did, and guess that road of life came up, and one fork went left, the other going right. Always easy to say which one's best after you've made the turn." Went on telling her he had it worked out, how they'd bypass Chicago and travel mainly at night, making their way down through Illinois, taking the back roads down to New Orleans. "Get them thinking we dropped right off the map."

"Really believe it'll throw them off?"

"Been working so far. We slip away and lie low, they'll forget us by and by."

Stella thinking if he said it often enough, maybe he'd believe it.

He went on about working up some new aliases, planned on buying a couple of cars that didn't cost too much, rent garages and park them here and there, have them all tanked up and ready to go.

He'd been in touch with his buddy Whitey, a guy he knew from working the prison library at The Walls, a guy fresh out on release. Not wanting to land back in that hell, Whitey put him in touch with Walt, another former inmate, a guy with a sick mother who could use the money Bennie was offering. Bennie wanting to buy a couple of clean guns, keep them in the stashed cars. Not wanting to walk into a gun shop himself, Bennie expecting the G-man had sent dodgers to every gun shop in the country.

. . . twenty-seven

DECEMBER 12, 1938

"Had my agents verify a couple unconfirmed sightings," Werner Hanni said into the phone, talking to the director. "Those newspaper stories turned up a mountain of witnesses, most of them proving false."

"I understand Agent Norris talked to Dickson's folks, tried to get them to talk reason to their boy, get him to turn himself in. Make it easy on himself."

Make it easy on *us*, Werner was thinking, saying, "Yes, sir. According to Gerald Norris, Dickson's old man claims the whole thing's a frame-up, told the papers law enforcement's out to get his boy."

"The man sounds like a communist."

"Well, he's getting some public sympathy from the sound of it."

"Norris got a memo from Bugas up in Detroit, that man doesn't consider the Dicksons dangerous, just a couple of Okie car thieves."

Werner guessing a memo like that made John Bugas another candidate for Anchorage.

"Suppose the man's got his opinion, but I want to hear what you've got to say, Hamm." Not letting Werner Hanni off the hook.

"Well, sir, though I'm not directly involved in the case . . ."

"I believe you mentioned that."

"I'd have to say the noose is tightening, sir." Werner reading from a sheet of paper, notes he'd written, anticipating this call. "Since Dickson's been charged with violation of the Dyer Act, the National Bank Robbery Act, plus three federal counts of kidnapping up around Detroit."

"And how about this *Bogus* saying they're not dangerous?"

"Well, I can't really answer to it, sir. Be best to ask him." Werner not feeling bad for John Bugas, had met him just the one time when they took down Karpis in New Orleans, got to know him on surveillance, and never took to the man.

"Yet with all these acts and charges, these Dicksons just go on terrorizing the country, doing it under the noses of my crack agents. Any idea of the flak I catch coming out of the Capitol?"

"Well, sir, Agent-in-Charge Guinane feels the end's coming, and from the—"

"Sounds like you people read from the same script, the same shit flowing out of the Kansas City office as yours."

"I can tell you I have my Aberdeen people compiling weekly information, sir, detailing everything we have on the Dicksons, updating the wanted posters, getting them out to the combined mailing—"

"Bank robbers at large and you're making posters."

"Six thousand of them, sir, photos of the couple going to every bureau office, post office, library, police station and sheriff's office in the country."

"Well, that's sounding more like a machine of justice. What else you got?"

"Well, sir, I had another look through Dickson's past, and turned up a former inmate Dickson was chummy with in the Missouri pen. A man named Whitey Kyle, recently released and living in St. Louis."

"You're thinking of springing a trap?"

"Sent a teletype to Agent-in-Charge Guinane, and he got hold of this ex-inmate and found out Dickson's been in touch, wanting to buy some guns."

"You could've told me that five minutes ago."

"Wanted to be sure before—" Werner Hanni heard the line go dead. Sitting back, letting go a long exhale. Then looking at the open file on his desk, the wanted poster he sent to Kansas City. Funny, feeling bad for Bennie Dickson and his teenage wife. From the photo Stella Mae didn't look like a killer, just a pretty girl who fell for the wrong guy, and just a few years older than his own daughter, at home and still fussing with her Raggedy Ann.

From his sheet, Bennie Dickson's temper landed him a parole violation in Topeka, back when he was still in his teens. One dumb move piled on another, and a lifetime of mistakes tumbled after. Taking a one-to-five fall for felony assault, Dickson served time in the reformatory in Hutchinson instead of going into the navy. Released to his parents' custody two years later, he stole a car with a couple of buddies from the reformatory, drove into Missouri and robbed the State Bank of Stotesbury. The dust they stirred fleeing the back roads made it easy for the local sheriff and his deputies. Deputies stated when they confronted Dickson, he took a missed swing at the sheriff, giving them cause to subdue him, banging up their prisoner. Werner Hanni wondered about a trained fighter swinging and missing. Trying to understand what caused a young man to turn like that — out just two months before he was back doing time in the Missouri State Pen, the bloodiest forty-seven acres in America, a hellhole overcrowded with defects. Pretty Boy Floyd among the inmates. The report said Dickson had been a model prisoner, earning merit time that knocked his sentence down to six years, released back into his father's custody.

Now here he was robbing and running with a young wife, right at the top of J. Edgar's shit list. Public enemies number and number two. Not vicious killers like Barrow or Dillinger, just mixed-up kids who robbed two banks in hard times. Didn't matter that nobody got hurt, Werner Hanni knew how law enforcement dealt with public enemies, didn't matter their age. The long arm would come down hard, and J. Edgar's press would spin a righteous outcome.

The best thing would be if Dickson's luck held, and they slipped into Canada or Mexico and just disappeared. Wouldn't be long and somebody new would catch the director's eye. Maybe some communist. And Werner hoped on his own luck, that the director would forget the name Werner Hanni, the man once dumb enough to offer his necktie instead of handcuffs.

twenty-eight

DECEMBER 25, 1938

"Dubbing us Bad Bennie and Sure Shot Stella. Got a ring to it, huh? Public enemies, that sound like us?" Bennie switched off the radio, been two months since the Brookings bank, but they were still making the news, with a manhunt going on. His smile faded, thinking of his old man hearing the same broadcast on Christmas, breaking his heart and giving up on thoughts of Bennie landing a career practicing law, ending up on the wrong side of it. Just a loser on a wanted dodger. One son with his name on a stone, and another with his name on the radio and his mugshot in the papers.

Stella had been thinking the same thing, the announcer on the radio calling them outlaws sought coast to coast. More shame and embarrassment on her family name. Could see Mother standing in her apron, stuffing a turkey, baking one of her pies, keeping busy with the festivities, not wanting to talk about it. Stella feeling bad for the letter Bennie had her write the beginning of the month, lying to her mother how Bennie had been shot to pieces at the Ace Motor Court, barely getting away and dying later. Wrote that she buried him down by the Missouri River, covered him with dirt and brush as best she could. Wrote that she was giving up this life of crime and taking a paying job with friends, changing her name and singing and dancing up someplace in Michigan. Asked her to pass on to Bennie's folks how she was sorry and that she'd stop and see them when she could. Wrote goodbye and don't worry, then signed it. The letter was postmarked Taylorville, Illinois. Bennie telling her it was the best way he could think of to hide their trail.

All of this hell started with what that awful man did to her, driving her home from the roller rink. Stella too young and dumb to say no thanks for the lift. If she took that ride home now, she'd put the .38 on the man. No curling up and crying, waiting for it to be over, that's for sure. She'd shoot him and tell him he had it coming, and she'd leave him bleeding and walk away, just like that. Maybe she would have done other things different too.

Sitting on opposite edges of the bed in that two-bit room, Stella and Bennie were quiet for a long time. The curtains were drawn, and she was thinking she must love him, remembering it was for better or worse, this being the worse part, and it was Christmas Day.

Sighing, he got up, sucking a Life Saver, moving like her grandpa, Stella guessing Bennie was still getting the spins and headaches. No point telling him again to go see a doctor. Sitting back down in the only chair in the place, he put his nose in the paper, ruffling the pages, saying, "Ought to get one of them news hounds to snap a photo of you aiming your big .38, show them the gun moll, what they're calling you. You see the one they got of Bonnie Parker? Got printed in all the dailies a bunch of times."

"Not the kind of acting I was hoping for, back when we talked of California." Stella looked at him, not sure if she was seeing him in a new way, one she wasn't so sure she liked.

"Her and old Clyde were just funning around, knowing how to have a good time." Bennie looked at her over the paper, asking what he had to do to catch a smile around here.

"Guess I'm just an old stick-in-the-mud."

"Hardly that. Fact, chief difference between you and Bonnie Parker, you're about twice as pretty."

"You mean after she got shot?"

Bennie laughed and pointed a finger at her. "Now there you go."

Stella swung around and faced him, tired of the clicking of the candy against his teeth, that sucking sound he kept making. Saying, "Man said they got lawmen from six states hunting us, closing in all the time." She reached and took the paper from him, folded it and dropped it to the floor.

"Say it to make the law look like they're getting things done."

"You ask me, sounds like we're part of a game, one for killers with badges. What's wrong with those people?"

"Like I been saying, we just got to keep 'em guessing." Bennie had been moving them from one town to the next, Excelsior Springs in Missouri, Conception, Rock Port, up to Beatrice, Nebraska, and winding back just outside Kansas City, changing names and cars and never staying anyplace more than a couple of days. If they got out at all, it was mostly at night, a couple of clubs, a walk across some empty field. "They sniff and get too close, then we got Sure Shot to blast out their tires."

"Feels like that, like they're getting too close."

"Those fools are looking where we've been, not where we're going to be. Definitely not where we are." Turning his head, he put a finger to the closed curtain, looked out past it. "We'll just slip right past them, same as always."

"And here we are, a one-room dump and it's Christmas."

"Well, lady, we'll be moving before the new year, working our way south just like I said. Taking you back to New Orleans. And soon the law'll forget about us on account we only did the two banks with nobody getting hurt, just the bankers' pride. Now let's make like it's Christmas, huh. What say, Sure Shot, we got any of those sandwiches left?"

Getting up, she went to the window, peeked past the curtains, saying, "You want the chicken or ham?"

"Hmm, let's see now . . . guess Bad Bennie'll go with the chicken, and how about a tin of that coffee to wash it down?"

"You even know the name of this place?"

Bennie shrugged. "It matter?"

"And the coffee . . . it's long cold."

"I don't mind it that way." He smiled, being patient with her. What he had left of the walking-around money wouldn't last them long in New Orleans. Not after sticking the eight hundred and fifty bucks in an envelope, the money he promised to Fred Stoufer up near Osage City for his Buick Model 60.

He'd need to sneak back to Topeka before long and dig up the rest of it, that or think about robbing another place. Wouldn't tell her if he did, and knowing if he came back anywhere near Topeka, she'd want to see her family. Bennie betting the family places would be under surveillance for some time. Getting up, he went to his jacket and fished in the pocket, taking out the ring box and holding it out. "You ask me, Bad Bennie and Sure Shot Stella's got a ring to it. What do you say?"

"Think you're—" Stopped, seeing him hold out the ring box.

"Here you go, lady. Merry Christmas." Smiling at the way her eyes lit up. "Surprised you, didn't I?"

. . . twenty-nine

JANUARY 3, 1939

"Can pay you for the lift." Bennie was looking at the man behind the wheel of the DeSoto, Bennie keeping his hand at his back pocket, putting on a smile.

"I bet you can, son. And I know who you are, and know you'd be paying me with bank money," the older man said, giving him that look, like he had Bennie pegged. Steadfast eyes of a veteran.

Bennie just smiled.

"You're them, ain't you, the ones in the paper?"

He could play it dumb, but the man knew who he was.

The middle-aged couple looked at each other on the front seat, the man telling his wife it would be alright.

"Just a couple in need of a lift, is all we are, nobody special," Bennie said, one hand still behind his back.

Stella stepped to the opposite window, smiling in at the wife, saying, "Hello."

The husband said, "Guess if I say no, you're gonna take your hand out that pocket, and ask me without the polite."

"Well, I could give you a song and dance, say you got us wrong ... but I can see you're too sharp for it." Bennie glanced up the street, where he'd seen the police cruiser turn, hoping the cop wasn't circling the block. Taking a chance, they'd come into town for a hot meal and coffee. Ditching the Studebaker down a drainage ditch, covering it with brush, he was keeping an eye for the right car, thinking this one would do the trick. A DeSoto Airflow with the split-screen windshield and a couple years on it. Never stole a DeSoto.

"Sharp enough to know we won't end up being pen pals writing letters."

Bennie shrugged, saying, "All we're after's a ride, mister. And if it helps, I'd be happy to pay for the ethyl, times being what they are."

"Well, how about you call me George, then, and this is Mamie. And how much ethyl are we talking about, son?"

Bennie grinned and took out what was left of his roll of bills, peeling off a couple.

Tucking away the bills, George patted Mamie's hand, telling her it would be alright.

Bennie and Stella got in the backseat, Bennie sitting behind George, glancing back to where he'd spotted the cruiser.

Driving off, George said, glancing back, "You mind me asking, you going by Ben and Stella Mae, or some other handles?"

"Right now you're talking to Johnny O'Malley," Bennie said, leaning an arm on the back of the seat. "And this here's . . ." Looking at Stella, winking. "You still Estelle?"

"On account Estelle O'Malley's got a nice ring," Stella said. "One I've grown fond of."

"Oh, yes, I think so too," Mamie said, half-turning to her. "Me, I'm christened Mary Claire, but everyone since Moses's been calling me Mamie."

"Well, Mamie, it's good to know you." Stella offered her hand, feeling the damp of the woman's hand. "You do like Johnny says, and things'll work out fine, nothing to worry about, and we can all be friends, and like he says, you'll come away a few dollars the richer."

"Well, guess that's fine then." Mamie forced up a smile, her lips trembling, her hand clutching her husband's.

"You got kids, Mamie?" Stella asked.

"Boy and a girl. Dorothy our oldest is in the motherly way, first grandchild's on the way, and Ben's off at school, studying to be a lawyer."

"Another Ben in the world, huh?" Bennie said. "Was thinking of being a lawyer myself. And might've if I hadn't got into banking." Winking at George, smiling at Mamie, liking that she smiled back.

"Guess life's full of turns and choices," George said, patting his wife's hand.

"More for some, but I figure Dame Fortune threw a few less my way. Not that I blame anybody for how it turned out, got no complaints." Reaching and taking Stella's hand. "My brother Spencer used to say I was born under what he called an Outlaw Moon. Not sure what he meant by it, but could be it explains why things turned out like they did."

"You really believe that, about Dame Fortune?" George said.

"Let's just say I learned to roll with the punches. But I tell you, George, I had the aptitude and the grades to make good, just I went the way of my true nature, you see what I'm saying? Top of that, there's the punches, and they seem to keep coming, trying to land."

"Well, maybe life's done you hard, son, but you always got choices, same as all of us. No offense."

"True enough, and I don't mean to sound like I'm complaining, just saying I'm doing what I see needs doing."

"Well, can hardly blame a fellow for it."

"You got kids, Estelle?" Mamie turned to Stella.

"Well, we haven't exactly had much time for planning it. What say, Johnny, we having kids?" She smiled at him.

"Sure we are, gonna fill a whole house." He winked at her.

"Well, that sounds real nice, and you two got lots of time for it, both plenty young. I mean, when you settle down."

"Yeah, hard to picture walking in a bank," Bennie said, "with a kiddie under one arm, saying this is a stickup, and asking if somebody's got a safety pin."

George smiled, squeezing Mamie's hand.

"Fellows I played pinochle with used to joke about it, robbing places, back when the drought first bit hard," George said. "Aside from the kidding, maybe I thought about it, what it would be like."

"You did not," Mamie said, slapping his arm. Telling him to keep his mind on the road.

"Thought they were kidding, but now I'm not so sure."

"Well, doesn't matter, thinking about it's one thing, and doing's another," Bennie said.

"Like I said, I hardly blame you for the way you went, son, times are tough," George said. "So, how far we taking you?" The end of town coming up.

"Well, how's the Indiana line sound?"

"Indiana, huh?" George took a glance at his gauge.

Reaching in a pocket, Bennie pulled his roll and stripped off a couple more bills, handing it forward. "A little something extra for your troubles."

"Well, not much trouble really; what say, Mother?"

"Nothing's pressing me," Mamie said.

"You mind me asking, what's it like?" George half-turned.

"You mean walking in and saying stick 'em up?" Bennie smiled.

"Sends a chill just thinking about it. Guess you need the nerve."

"Well, sir, guess it's not suited for everyone. And that chill you're talking about, it comes and kind of balls up the bottom of your stomach, at least it does the first time."

"Can't imagine it," Mamie said.

"Once you go in and you pull, that's it, there's no turning around." Bennie was in his element. "Sure no time for wool-gathering, everything rushing by at train speed, and you got to stay sharp, dealing with it as it plays, you know? The whole world at the end of your pistol."

George shook his head, "Gonna be something, just telling I had you in my car. I mean, if that's alright to say?"

"Oh sure," Bennie said, going on, "It's like this job you got to do, getting the ones on the other side of the wicket to believe you mean it. It's not the look at the gun, but the look in the eye that gets them emptying the cash drawers."

"Read about the time lock on the one bank," George said.

"Time locks on both banks. Was a bit of bad luck, but like I said, just had to roll with it. Reason some papers called us the time-lock bandits, how we kept cool under pressure."

"That back before they called you Bad Bennie and Sure Shot Stella?"

"That's right. Called me Bad Bennie on account of a stretch I did. Sure Shot got her name for popping out the tire of the patrol car bearing down on us, cops firing from behind with intent to kill. Did what she had to do, *bam bam*, just like that, and they were gone."

George nodded to Stella like he was impressed, then said to Bennie, "There's a Mobil up the block, that be alright?"

"Any kind you want, George, that's fine by me."

Stella eyed the Mobil station, not much more than a shack with the tin signs nailed to the walls, a stack of tires out front by the single pump, a garage with the wood door hanging open on one hinge. Slipping her hand in her bag, she watched past the shadows and inside that garage door.

Bennie got out with George, asking how far their place was, not looking concerned, not like it could be an ambush.

The attendant was no more than a kid coming out the garage door, wiping his hands on an oil rag, asking George what he could do for him.

"I could stand a visit to the ladies'. That be alright?" Mamie turned on the seat, asking Stella.

"You got to go, you got to go," Stella said. "Not sure they got one, maybe just a back house."

Nodding, Mamie got out, asking the attendant about it, being directed to the side.

"You want me to go with her?" Stella said to Bennie out the window.

"She's alright," Bennie said, seeing the attendant looking for the filler cap, pointed it out for him, then got back to talking to George, asked how he liked the Airflow.

George calling her a good old girl.

Getting back in, Bennie said to Stella, "You keep worrying, lady, you're gonna give yourself the shakes." Bennie spotting the cruiser turning onto the main drag a block ahead.

Stella reached in her bag.

"Easy." He watched the car come, the same cop in the patrol car, glancing over at the DeSoto, giving a wave to George. Bennie looking down at the floor.

Turning, she watched the patrol car roll down the block, finally turning off. "Think he'll be back?"

"Guess we'll see." Bennie got back out.

The attendant took the nozzle from the filler, looking at the pump display and telling George, "That'll be a buck fifty."

Whistling, George handed him a couple of bills, Mamie coming from around the side of the building, past the stack of tires, getting in the passenger door.

The attendant saying he'd be right back with the change and going into the garage.

"Forget the change," Bennie called, telling George to get in the back, saying he wouldn't mind giving her a try, not waiting on a reply, getting behind the wheel.

The attendant was coming back out, counting the change as Bennie drove off, the kid watching as they pulled away, then looked at the money in his hand.

... *thirty*

JANUARY 3, 1939

"Think they'll talk?"

"Don't think they can help it. Tell folks they just rubbed up to the famous Dicksons, how we made them drive us out of state, likely throw in we did it at gunpoint. Be enough story there for a lifetime." Bennie watched the DeSoto disappear up the road.

"Just can't believe we didn't take their car."

"Told him we just needed a lift. You heard the man say it's his pride and joy."

"Well, would you looky here, Bad Bennie is going soft, standing out here with no car in the middle of town. Waving off two live witnesses, could be they'll talk it over and end up going right to the police station."

"Won't matter much. Told them we're heading to Ann Arbor." Bennie aiming to head through Memphis and down to New Orleans, eventually out to the coast. Guessing he had about a half hour before the cops came in force, he turned back to the Evansville Motors car lot they'd passed, getting an idea and saying, "Come on." Taking her hand.

"What're we doing?"

"Gonna go kick some tires."

"Middle of town, and you want to swipe a car?"

"Nope, I'm gonna buy one."

"Why'd we do that?"

"Dials down the heat; plus I got this walking-around money, and guess I just like the feel of it, and like to haggle and buy one off the lot for a change." Smiling, telling her except for getaway cars and the ones he bought cheap and stashed in garages, he'd hardly ever bought one that was just for him. There was the new Buick Century he bought off the lot, drove twenty miles and rolled like a tin can, yeah, it was a shame about that one. Guessing he'd never tell her the whole story about it.

Slinging his arm around her shoulder, he told her she was the best girl in the world, carrying the suitcase, everything they owned inside it, and walked them under the Authorized Chrysler/Plymouth Dealer sign. Another sign said all it took was a small down payment.

A string of bulbs hung over the line of Chryslers, Fords and Chevrolets lined like a wall out front. Bennie pointed at another sign: "If the horn blows, we'll buy it." Grinning at that, he ran a hand along the fender of an Airflow, this one a Chrysler.

Stella saying she liked the color.

Bennie saying it went with her eyes, except they'd stick out in a pale-blue-colored car. "Plus, I got no use for a four-door. Not yet, anyway." Winking at her, back to thinking about having kids someday. Then saying, "I got my mind set on a coupe, something black or dark blue, doesn't stick out, but something with a look, you know. And, of course with a V8, and be okay if it had whitewalls. How about this one, she's a beaut, huh?" Stepping between the row of cars, looking in the window of a Duesenberg Torpedo, eight years old, "mint condition" painted on the windshield.

"We afford it?" Looking at the price painted on the windshield.

"Guess you never heard me haggle?"

"With or without a gun?"

"Be something, huh, driving to New Orleans with the top down, the wind blowing our hair?"

Stella said yeah, getting a picture of it, something she'd seen in a magazine somewhere, a movie star with her hair blowing in a convertible.

"Yeah, and maybe sometime we will." Bennie thinking better of it. Too easy to get spotted, and not much protection in a ragtop. Guessing George and Mamie were discussing going to the station house about now, dying to tell what happened.

"Help you folks?" The man had a wide smile and a loud suit, angling between a pair of Plymouths, the door to the tiny sales office open behind him. Saying to Bennie, "You been in before, sure I seen you?"

"Long time back maybe." Bennie not saying it had been in a younger day, and after hours, when the place was closed up, helped himself to a Chevy coupe that time, joyriding in it for three days before crumpling its fender and abandoning it against a stone fence. The highway patrol finding it the next day, coming to question him.

"Can see you're a man of style," the salesman said, patting the nearest Plymouth, then extending his hand. "Harvey Declan. Here to serve."

"Joe Trent, here to buy, and this here's the missus."

Harvey did the hello routine, a delight to meet them, what a fine day it was. Led them down a row, past a Nash in white.

Saying he was in kind of a hurry, Bennie was thinking he'd never swiped a Nash before, liking the look of it, thinking the Ambassador with its straight-eight might be worth wiring up sometime.

"What's the scoop on this girl?" Bennie eyed a two-door coupe in black with gray down the sides. Parked at the end of the line. Looking underneath her, checking for a puddle of oil.

"The Dictator. Well, Joe, I can see you do have an eye, a man who knows his cars. And you can see this one's got the batwing," Harvey said, going around and pointing to the back split-window. "And she's got a trunk you could hide a body in." Laughing.

"Well, let's hope it won't come to that," Bennie said, smiling and pointing to the price on the windshield. "I'm betting that's a misprint, Harvey."

"I know you're joking around, Joe. And I bet you know a thing or two. Don't need to tell you she's a steal for eight hundred. And when the boss ain't looking, I'll throw in a spare tire."

"That'd be fine, Harvey, and I'm not sure right now, which one of us you figure's doing the stealing."

"That's a good one, Joe." Harvey laughed, showing his good nature, and popped open the car door, leaned far enough to look at the instruments behind the steering. "See here, got the low mileage. The tires are pretty fair, just go on and kick 'em. Car like this over in Louisville goes for over eleven hundred."

"Brand new, maybe, but this girl's been round the block a bunch of times. And *hmm*, I'm thinking two hundred's fair and square."

"Well, Joe, for that money I can let you have, let's see . . ." He looked over the tops of his fleet, tightened his lips, kind of doubtful. "You know, I got nothing for that. Closest thing's a Ford truck out back, could go as low as say . . . two-fifty. Needs some work, but runs good once you get her started."

Checking his pocket watch, Bennie glanced around, turning to an older Buick Century. If the Dictator was a race horse, then this was the mule. High mileage with some rust starting to show from underneath, Bennie asking what was under the hood, then saying, "How about I give you the two for this one, and take my chances."

"Well now . . ." Harvey looked down, shuffling his feet, good at playing the game, seeing the man was getting edgy. "I'd love to sell her to you, Joe, honest I would, but I'm sure you understand, I got a bottom-line situation here, and uh, two bills, well, that's not gonna cut it, not even close. How about if I were to shave off . . . *hmm* . . . let's see . . ." Rolling his eyes, Harvey looked pained, thinking hard. "Rock bottom's uh . . . four-fifty, how'd that be?"

"Half as good as three-fifty."

"I hear what you're saying, Joe, sure I do — times are tough and money's tight, got to hold it in two fists, I get that, believe me, goes the same for all of us." Harvey glanced at the green in Bennie's hand, saying, "Afraid four and a quarter's the best I can do."

Looking at him a moment longer, Bennie never changed his expression, then reached in a pocket and drew out two hundred more dollars that he'd peeled off before he even walked onto the lot, kept it in his front pocket. Counting it out between his thumb and forefinger, doing it slow and before holding out the four hundred, knowing he had him, but remembering the cops could be coming along anytime, then again maybe George and Mamie were made of better stuff. Saying, "And Harvey, I'm gonna want her topped with ethyl."

Harvey looked at the bills in the man's hand, and swallowed hard.

... *thirty-one*

MARCH 7, 1939

"And a direct line to the director, well, how about that?" Werner Hanni felt relief, the director hadn't called him in over two weeks.

"Yeah, it feels like I've gone right to the top." Gerald B. Norris sounded pleased with himself.

Werner Hanni thinking that could mean straight to Anchorage, top of the world with ice and blowing snow, thanking God that Gerald was the SAC of the case. Hoover giving him his direct number, wanting daily reports. The Dicksons had flown off the radar since the beginning of the year, two eyewitnesses sighting them in Oklahoma City. Nothing since then.

"Now if only we'd get an eyeball on them," Gerald said, trying to sound enthused. Had G-men looking into sightings of the Dicksons in Maine one day, and California the next. All the tips proving false and taking vast manpower hours. Hoover demanded his reports, wanting all offices involved and open day and night, every day of the week until they put a stop to what he called "the Dickson menace."

Two months of false sightings, the pair eluding the entire bureau, Hoover's crack agents scrambling at every lead. A damned embarrassment.

At the director's insistence, Norris dispatched teams of field agents to Taylorville, had them roll up their sleeves and dig up the banks of the river where Stella Mae's intercepted letter to her mother claimed she had buried Ben Dickson's body. The director believed Dickson had been mortally wounded at the Ace Motor Court gun battle, all those shots fired into that garage. Probing the banks, searching for a shallow grave, Norris's agents moved from the bridges and banks of Taylorville, checking all the bridges in all nearby towns, taking over a month of digging to turn up nothing. The shovels were put back in the shed after John Bugas, the SAC at the Detroit office, noted an overlooked but confirmed report stating the Dicksons were spotted in Michigan a week after Stella's letter to her mother. Hoover yelling some more about this teenage girl making fools of the whole bureau.

Betting there was a good chance Dickson had been injured at the Ace Motor Court, Werner Hanni had taken the initiative, sending thousands of posters to doctors, hospitals and clinics. Expanding on the idea, and getting circulars to every camp owner, boxing promoter, gas station owner and pharmacist in the country. Playing postal service, Werner Hanni kept his office compiling all new information and dispatching it to all the offices. Something that actually pleased the director.

"Well, with the pressure we're putting on them, all they can do is run, and they can't do that forever," Norris said. "That chase at Thanksgiving went down as attempted murder on a couple of peace officers."

"The teenage girl shooting out a tire?" Hanni said.

"Point is, the patrol car crashed, sending both officers in need of medical attention, their car a total wreck. Then they stole a car and took hostages across state lines, only one way to deal with that kind."

"What kind, a teenage girl?"

"Armed and dangerous felons. Don't matter the age. The director's got a mind to sweep up both families for aiding and abetting to boot. Helping them hide out and with-holding information."

"You staking them out?"

"Their houses, the family farm, the cabin by the lake. Got eyes on all the places. Dickson's not leaving an easy trail, but it's just a matter of time."

"Public enemy, a sixteen-year-old girl. You got kids, Gerald?"

"Nope, and a word to the wise, Werner, it's talk like that'll get the director thinking you're not playing like part of the team."

"And I guess you got the hunger, Gerald, making you the right man." Werner thinking the man's idea of wanted results would end with two more felons face down. And if the Dicksons stayed gone, there could be sled dogs and parkas in Gerald Norris's future.

... *thirty-two*

APRIL 6, 1939

"Told you, her name's Naomi. Sister of this guy Walt, friend of this guy I knew in The Walls."

"Yeah, I know, you told me. Friend of this Whitey." Stella looking out at the countryside flashing by.

"They're guys I can count on."

"A guy you're paying."

"Walt's got a sick mother, and he can use a few bucks."

"Can't help it, I got a bad feeling ..."

"Got to do this now, huh?" Bennie frowned.

Stella sitting in the Ford they just traded for the Chrysler, her hair dyed brown. That bad feeling had been growing since they left the upstairs place across from Audubon Park, coming north again.

She'd been happy in New Orleans, felt safe there. Except for longing to see her family, she'd never come north again. Bennie insisting they come to dig up more money. So she gave up the warm breezes and going by Mrs. Robert Kane, and she gave up that front porch where she loved to rock and watch couples stroll by with their kids, folks walking their dogs. Jazz filling the air, mixing with the smell of shrimp frying. Dancing and voodoo and not-a-care, and shotgun houses and Mardi Gras down in the Quarter. Learning tennis and driving golf balls. Bennie registering as Robert Kane at Tulane University, thinking again about that law degree. Dressing up and hitting the night spots: the Cat and Fiddle and Tyler's Garden.

She longed to put down roots, tired of moving place to place, changing her name more than her socks, wanting to leave the running behind. Liked him being easy, like he was that long-ago day when they met at the roller rink. Wanting him to get back to writing poetry and reading his books by Karl Marx and H.G. Wells and poking his nose into *Mein Kampf*, telling her about Adolf Hitler and his Beer Hall Putsch, halfway round the world, saying now there was a true lunatic.

He had pinned up her photo from the *Liberty* magazine on the kitchen wall, the feature on the gun moll, Stella Mae Dickson, a girl who liked shooting as much as she liked roller skating. He'd tossed the magazine with the papers piled on top a box of dynamite sticks.

Stella said it wasn't her best side, but she liked her hair the way it had been, still blonde then, the photo nearly two years old and peeled from her mother's family album. She knew New Orleans had taken most of their cash, and they had to get to Kansas, the farmhouse and Ben's cabin, dig up what he buried there.

"Well, you know how I feel about it."

"Yeah, you made it plain enough. Just a quick stop with a chance to make a call to the folks, then we'll be back here before you know it."

Stella imagined cops and FBI bothering her folks and still keeping an eye on the house, keeping up their manhunt, they'd never give up.

He was frowning and asking, "What's crawled up your shorts, huh?"

"Could be the change of life maybe."

"Yeah, at sixteen?"

"This life's making me old before my time." Then saying she was sorry she said it.

Bennie laughed. "Can get you some salts, you want, lady. Look, I don't want to leave myself, and it'll just be a bit longer."

"You been saying that since Elkton. Just exactly how long's this bit?"

"Till we're on the other side of it."

"Other side, hope you're not thinking like heaven."

Grinning, Bennie said she was one funny girl. "Gonna get our money, pick up some guns, then get our tails back down south." Asking her what they called them little crabs they had down in the Quarter.

"Crawdads, you know what they're called. And what do we need with more guns?"

"Yeah, crawdads. Remember how you sucked them down. Why you guess they call 'em that?"

"I know what you're doing," she said, calling him Johnny.

"Yeah, what's that?"

"Playing me, like I'm some dummy."

"I don't think that, and you know it."

"Tell me something else nice. I could use it."

"Like what?"

"I don't know, like something about our life, how it's gonna be."

"We're going to have that nice house, just got to decide between New Orleans — the food, the music — or we got Los Angeles, with fruit hanging on every tree, Warner Brothers and RKO and all that." He didn't mention what he'd read about more migrant camps springing up, how the Okies were being turned back at gunpoint at the state line, finding out there was no more work than there was anyplace else.

"You really think I could do it, be any good up on the screen, act like I'm somebody else?"

"Think you'd be a natural, like that Carole, uh . . ."

"Lombard?"

"That one, yeah, and or uh, Olivia de Havilland. Man, she's a dish, huh?"

"Hey, watch it." Play slapping his arm, thinking her mother would sooner see her up on the screen than in the papers, and could be proud of her for a change. "Sure would be something, huh?"

"Yeah, and hey, you get tired of the bright lights, we'll just head right back across the Pontchartrain, settle down there."

"So, what's this about guns?"

"Yeah, don't worry yourself about it. Just a good thing to keep around, keeps us safe. Oh, I tell you I was thinking of taking flying lessons, what say to that?"

"I think you could be part nuts."

"Yeah, I called this place, the Jones School of Flying. Just picture it, the two of us robbing a place and making our getaway, flying right out of sight and stumping the G-man, putting them at oh-and-three. How's that sound?"

"Just finished saying we were done with it."

"Yeah, I'm just having fun with you."

"For sure you're part nuts, the other part's crazy."

"Crazy in love or crazy like a fox?" Giving her a wink.

"Let you know when I figure it out."

"I bet old Clyde or even Dillinger never thought of doing it like that. Bank robbing down from the sky, swooping and landing right on the main drag, taking them by surprise, and flying right over the roadblocks. Stumping the G-man again."

"Land your plane on Main Street and wait for the time locks, huh?"

"Man, I hate them things, still can't believe our luck."

"You really gonna learn to fly?"

"Well, I was thinking it till I learned this Jones School charges six hundred bucks for it, you believe it?"

She whistled, looking surprised.

"There you go, you did it."

She whistled again, delighted with herself.

"Anyway, I told them what they could do with their fee, a true bunch of crooks."

☾

Heading to St. Louis, he was back to doing most of the driving, the dizziness gone now, driving mostly at night, stealing a Mercury outside of Fayetteville, calling his prison buddy Walt, the ex-con living in St. Louis now, telling Bennie he could get him a couple of handguns, told him how much, said he'd have them next day. Bennie told him that would be fine, then driving north to the family farm, keeping low and moving along that tree line alone, digging up the money, feeling like a grave robber, working in the middle of the night, their walking-around cash nearly gone. Going back to the car a quarter mile back, he decided to leave what he had stashed from the Brookings job by the railcar just outside of Topeka. He'd come back for it another time.

They slept the rest of the night in the Mercury, then drove east to St. Louis. Forest Park and the brick buildings of the busy midtown flashing past, Stella caught sight of the Yankee System Hamburger Shop with its yellow awning, couldn't see anybody inside as they passed, Bennie seeing a barber shop across the street, thinking he could use a trim. Looking for a parking spot, saying, "You believe the traffic in this town?" Seeing a car pull away from the curb, down the block on Euclid, Bennie pulling into it.

"A guy you did time with, huh?"

"Already told you all that. Meeting his sister, in case somebody's watching him." He looked at her. "What's wrong now?"

"Well, how you sure you can trust him, this guy Walt?"

"Got to start right now, huh?"

"Told you, I got this feeling."

"You spend time in The Walls, you learn not to snitch."

"That like a blood oath?"

"The blood part, yeah, that's for sure." Bennie sounding annoyed with her.

"Okay, but you're meeting his sister, one you never seen before."

Bennie sighed. "Doing it this way in case somebody's got an eye on Walt. Like insurance. Look, his sister's a nurse, knows nothing about why she's meeting me, just needs money for the sick mother. Knows I'm handing her some cash, helping out my friend Walt. And she's gonna give me a key to this place, that's all. Not gonna be any eyes on her."

"It's his family, not yours."

"Lady, how about you give it a rest, huh? Your mind's playing tricks, all this driving we been doing, and tell you the truth, you're getting my nerves jumping." He drew air, pushed up a smile, looked like he was sorry he said it.

"I'm allowed to ask questions."

"Yeah, lots of them."

"Okay, besides being a nurse, what else you know about this Naomi?"

"Not gonna let it go, huh?"

"Nope."

"Alright . . . I know she'll be wearing a black hat. Gonna be sitting at the counter by the front. Gonna hand her the money, and she's handing me a key. That's it. Maybe get something to eat, had nothing since that place this morning. How about you? You want something? Hamburger's five cents."

"Yeah, I guess so."

"Want it with cheese?"

"Why not surprise me the way you do."

"Picking up a key, for Christ's sake. We'll lie low a day or so, then breeze right out of here. Finish waiting till the heat dies down."

"Ain't no heat up here." She wrapped her arms around herself.

He leaned across the seat and pecked her cheek. "Stop the worrying, okay? Reaching under her seat, taking the .38 he gave her and tucked it behind his back.

"Where's yours?"

"Put it in the trunk."

"Could come with you, now I can whistle."

"You just sit tight and keep this buggy running, and the hat low." He put a hand to her shoulder and squeezed, said he loved her. Buttoning the flannel jacket, he put on his new hat and walked off with that easy swagger.

Cranking the window halfway down, she called after him, "And go easy on the onions."

Feeling the evening chill coming, she watched him in the side mirror, going up the block and into the Yankee System. Part of her wanted to follow him, didn't matter what he said. Then telling herself she was being a nag, she slid across the seat and got behind the wheel, sitting there with the engine running, and tried to whistle. Couldn't wait to get out of there, thinking about that upstairs place by Audubon Park.

The pistol shots made her jump, and she just sat there, staring straight ahead, her hands tight on the wheel, her fingernails digging into her palms. Turning on the seat, she saw a man standing over something far up the block, the shape of another man on the ground, three more men running from the barbershop across the street.

And she was crying, wanted that swagger and that smile, wanting him to tell her she was being an old nanny and there was nothing to worry about. Just went to see a woman named Naomi. Then she saw the woman in the black hat coming out of the place. Didn't look at the man on the ground or the four lawmen, the woman just walked right past the Mercury. Stella watching her go, the paper bag of money in her hand. The bag Bennie gave her. And Stella reached under the seat for the .38 that wasn't there. Stopped herself from yelling and going after her.

Just sat there crying until a man came walking with his dog, coming the opposite way and looking in at her, asking if she was alright. Then a distant siren was screaming.

And she cranked the key on the already running engine, shifted gears, the car jolting forward and slamming into the next car's bumper. A police cruiser raced fast down the street, its siren blaring and lights flashing. Sure they had her pinned in the parking spot, she threw up her hands as the car whizzed by — two cops inside, neither looking over.

Leaning into her window, the man with the dog asked if she was sure she was alright.

"I'm a woman, you know we can't drive, right?" Then, wiping at her eyes, putting her foot on the clutch, she backed up, moved the stick the way Bennie showed her, gave it gas and turned the car around in the street amid the honking and drove past the hamburger place. Another siren wailed from another direction.

Slowing, she couldn't get herself to look over but knew it was him face down on the sidewalk, in that plaid jacket. In her mind, she was going to the rendezvous, where she'd wait for him. Remembered old Johnny O'Malley calling himself unkillable, couldn't be beat. Seeing him getting away like he did at the Ace Motor Court, forty-eight shots fired into the garage and he crashed out of there. Remembered the way he said, "Call me lucky." And had her believing it.

. . . *thirty-three*

APRIL 7, 1939

Werner Hanni was leaning back in the chair, arms behind his neck, thinking the director hadn't been calling much, feeling off the hook. One of the agent trainees walked past the open door, leaned in and slid the newspaper across his desk.

"Looks like they got him." Clement Lemke had a long neck and curly hair, more the look of a country bumpkin than a G-man in training, but Werner guessed the kid showed the right promise.

He looked at the front of the *Globe-Democrat*.

Clement saying, "At some hamburger joint in St. Louis."

Hanni grabbed the paper and read: Topeka desperado beaten to the draw. The photo of Bennie Dickson laid out on a St. Louis sidewalk. Four federal agents armed with pistols and rifles standing over the body of the outlaw no older than the trainee on the other side of his desk. Special-Agent-in-Charge Gerald Norris was looking at the camera, quoted as saying, "We got him or he would have got us."

Werner Hanni guessed Norris and his goon squad stood there spinning the story as the sirens closed in, forgetting about Stella Mae, most wanted number two on J. Edgar's shit list, same way the Topeka police and Shawnee county deputies did at the Ace Motor Court.

She was likely waiting in a stolen car nearby, maybe watched it happen. The article went on how Dickson was armed to the teeth with a Colt .45 and a snub-nosed .38, the article saying he had a smoking one in each hand. Werner betting if there were any guns, the ambulance attendants found them in Dickson's waistband when they carted away the body. Saying to Clement, "How's it a gunfight when the man doesn't even draw his piece?"

"Says they beat him to it, sir."

"So, somehow facing them, drawing on them, he took two in the back?"

"Well, could be he fired and turned to run, went chicken."

"Could be you need to learn to read between the lines, son. Learn that sometimes stories get sanitized before the ink's dry."

"Yes, sir." Clement Lemke looked doubtful, like he'd never considered it.

"This was a man who never shot anybody, waiting on two time locks to pop." Hanni scanned the article; it went on how the agents had no choice but to return fire. Hanni building the real story: how Norris and his men lay in ambush, a couple of them in the alley that showed behind them in the photo, the others somewhere across the street, likely at the barbershop waiting till Dickson walked from the hamburger joint. The ones in the alley likely got jumpy and put him down as he passed — Werner guessing it was Bush, the rookie standing next to Norris, the kid not knowing any better — not giving Dickson a chance to give himself up. Betting the director liked the outcome: another public menace wiped off the map by federal agents left with no choice. Ending in righteous headlines, and saving the bureau further embarrassment.

Whoever fired the shot, Gerald Norris would get a pat on the head. The article citing how the local cops were called to the scene, arresting the four G-men, one of the officers saying later they looked like gangsters. Threw them in lock-up until the mess was cleared up.

Smiling at the thought, Hanni guessed the director would spit about that part, when he read how two local cops arrested and locked up four of his finest, G-men with jurisdiction coast to coast. But in the end, they had a job to do and they did it, the criminal was dispatched in the act of pulling his weapons. The G-men not apologizing for doing the job. The press going along with it, calling it a righteous shooting.

"Says an eyewitness at the barbershop claims a woman in black walked out of the burger joint right after the shots were fired, stepped past them and just disappeared," Clement Lemke said. "Reminds me of the woman in red, the one who helped get Dillinger. Guess you land yourself at the top of the list, good chance you're gonna end up like that."

"Except they forgot the wife again, always right there with him."

"Sure Shot Stella? Well, guess so, but I wouldn't want to be in her shoes."

"Guess you wouldn't. Be funny, an FBI man in a woman's shoes."

Clement's cheeks flushed, but he smiled at the joke, saying, "Suppose if she resists, our boys'll do for her. Won't matter she's a woman. Same as Bonnie Parker, and that Ma Barker. Ice water in their veins, women like that."

Werner Hanni nodded, thanked him for the paper and watched him go back to his desk, thinking back to his last phone call with Gerald B. Norris, guessing in spite of their bungling and letting Stella Mae Dickson drive right past his agents, the SAC would likely be in line for a promotion, at least a bigger office. Anchorage not in that man's future.

And with any luck the name of Werner Hanni would fade entirely from the director's mind. Then he was wondering what other line of work was out there for a former G-man. Maybe a private detective, or a bodyguard out in Hollywood, a lot of bodies in need of guarding out there.

... *thirty-four*

APRIL 7, 1939

The pistol shots rang around in her sleep, Stella waking in a sweat. As soon as she'd heard the shots, she knew what it meant. Remembering his words: if anything went wrong, just drive out of there and meet back at Ben's cabin outside of Topeka. She considered going there and hiding out, but knew he wasn't coming back this time.

After it happened, she turned the car around on the street, a delivery driver honking his impatience. Driving past the burger place, she saw him face down, the two police holding pistols on the G-men, their hands in the air. Wanting to stop the car and run to Bennie and hold him. Thinking maybe he wasn't gone. Tears flowed, Stella sniffed and switched on the windshield wipers, turned them back off, realizing it wasn't raining. Then she drove to the far side of town, stopping when she saw the sign for a garage for rent.

Unable to drive on, she pulled herself together and went to the door, deciding between Emma Duncan and Frances Cameron. Said she was Frances when the man opened the door, interested in his garage for rent. Paid him the three dollars and parked the car in the garage out back, then when the man disappeared in the house, she crawled on the backseat, curling up with her coat for a blanket and cried herself dry. A fitful night of hearing those shots every time she nodded off. Giving up on sleep, she sat in the dark with her knees up, trying to feel him around her, guessing if there was a heaven he'd be waiting when her time came. And guessing if she kept acting dumb it could come pretty soon.

By morning, she decided to get out of there, the lawmen would be searching for her, Stella feeling a longing to go to her mother. Didn't matter the FBI men would be watching the house. When the city began to wake she got out, smoothing her dress and finger-combing her brown-dyed hair, slipped on her coat and hat, took the suitcase and left the garage, the night giving way to the sounds of morning, a milk truck going by, lights coming on inside houses, people getting ready for a day of work.

Leaving Bennie's Mercury, she headed through town, passing a newspaper box, not allowing herself to glance at the morning edition, knowing how the headline would read. Trying to shake away that image of Bennie down on that sidewalk, afraid she'd never get it out of her head. All she wanted right then was to go home to Mother.

Maybe she'd come back for the Mercury sometime, had paid for the garage for three months. The man saying he'd keep the car in running order, check on the battery and tires.

Walking the city streets, she hailed a cab and had the driver take her to the airport, saw a couple of uniformed cops outside the doors, didn't like the way they were watching the people going in the place. Saying she changed her mind, she had the driver turn around, remembering a travel office Bennie had driven past yesterday.

Walking into Longo Travel, Stella looked at the two men on either side of a big desk, both in suspenders with their sleeves rolled up. Stepping in, she told the one on the far side facing her she wanted to hire a driver to take her to Kansas City. The nameplate on the desk told her she was talking to Mike.

"Well, it's your lucky day, miss, Artie Hoffman here's making a run today. You got room for one more, Artie?"

"Sure I do." Turning to her, Artie said it was three bucks on a split-fare, meaning there would be other passengers. "Be about a four-hour ride." Then Artie told her to come back at four thirty sharp.

She paid the fare up front, gave a nervous look out the window, seeing a patrol car go past. Wishing she had the .38 in the bottom of her bag. Leaving, she looked in a few shop windows, watching the reflections for anybody coming up on her.

Seeing the post office, she went in, past a wanted dodger of her and Bennie, somebody scratching out his likeness with a pencil. Stella feeling the weight, the realization of never seeing him again was slow in coming. Stella forcing herself not to cry and draw attention to herself.

Holding back seventy dollars, she tucked the rest of the money she was carrying in a package — the money Bennie had dug up — not even counting it, writing Liz's name and address as best she remembered it. Scratching a note for her friend Liz to hang on to it, hoping she could count on her. Putting the rest of the cash in her bag, along with a poem Bennie wrote, she wished she had one of the photos — the one of the two of them at the Topeka Free Fair back in the fall — afraid what he looked like would start to fade. There wouldn't be any leather-bound photo albums, no kids playing in the yard, no New Orleans, no Los Angeles.

And she cried again, reciting the lines he wrote, swearing she would never forget them:

> *In the eyes of men I am not just,*
> *But in your eyes, O life, I see justification*
> *You have taught me that my path is right if I am true to you.*

Cried most of that day, the worst one of her life. Got coffee to keep warm, and forced herself to eat a sandwich at a diner, later on she couldn't remember what she ate. Got back early to the travel office. The one called Artie was alone in the office, looked like he might have been drinking, his eyes red-rimmed and his hair in need of a comb.

"I'm parked out front," he said, pointing to the old Buick, a four-door with faded paint and rusting side panels. "You got bags, I can put them in back for you."

"No, just this one."

Artie told her they were waiting on another passenger, then got busy working on some paperwork.

"How long we got to wait?"

"Be anytime now. I'm sorry for it, but hardly worth driving all the way to Kansas City for the one fare."

"Said I'm going to Topeka."

"Sure you said Kansas City, miss."

"Well, I'm sure I didn't." Getting agitated, she tried to keep her voice even.

"Well, my mistake then. Guess either one's fine, just Topeka's a dollar more." Artie shrugged, looked at her, then said to forget about the extra fare, going on and making small talk about the dust storms that swept across the Plains, killing crops and folks, then asked how she liked it here in St. Louis.

"Can't stand this place, no offense." She looked out the window, hoping to end the chitchat, too tired for it.

Artie finished up the paperwork, and she paced between the desk and the window, her bag in her hand. In spite of having her coat on, she couldn't get warm after the night on the backseat, spending most of the day walking city streets. Too afraid to go back and hide in the rented garage, just in case the FBI men had found the car.

"So, you traveling on your own, huh?"

"Come here visiting some friends."

"And Topeka's home?"

"Uh huh, staying at my folks' place."

"Well, don't mean to poke in nobody else's business, but a girl like you in a town like this, all on her own . . ." Artie shook his head, saying, "St. Louis ain't the safest place for a girl, the things that been going on here."

"Well, I can look out for myself, and like I said, I got friends, and an uncle here."

"Then I guess you know this town's got its rusty side. Sorry, I don't mean to give you frights. Just, maybe you heard about the FBI bringing down the most the wanted man in the country, just yesterday. Right over town, about the time I finished supper."

Stella shook her head, looking out the window, willing herself not to cry again.

"Well, surprised you ain't heard. All anybody's talking about it, any place you go. Bennie Dickson's done, every lawman after him for a year or more. Good to know we got fellows like the FBI men, keeping us safe. Caught up with this Dickson out of the Yankee burger joint, told him to put up his hands, but I guess he had his own ideas. The way they think, the criminal mind, you know?"

"No, I wouldn't know."

"I guess not. Funny, if I'd heard the shots from my place, would've thought it was a truck backfiring, you know, the way they do?"

Looking out the window, she tried to hold it together.

"Uh, I'm sorry, miss. Can see I'm upsetting you. Guess it's not something a young girl cares to talk about."

"I guess not."

Artie going on anyway. "Well, rest assured, miss, that big chief, uh . . ." Snapping his fingers. "Hoover, the man says he's cleaning up, and I guess I believe him. Won't be a gangster left before that man's looking at his gold watch. Doing a heck of a job too, letting a decent man make a living and rest easy in between."

"Said you weren't gonna talk about it." She stopped from biting her lip, thinking this was going to be the longest four hours of her life.

"Yeah, you're right. So, uh, whereabouts in Kansas City?"

"What?"

"Where you want to be dropped?"

"Topeka."

"Right, sorry, Topeka."

Her fingers were curled, her nails digging into the meat of her hands. She was back to thinking about that woman in the black hat, coming out of the burger place, the nurse with the sick mother Bennie was helping out, walking past him on that sidewalk. Didn't even give him a look.

Artie asking directions, for when they got into Topeka.

"Don't know all the street names, but I'll know the turns when I see them."

"Sure, that'll be fine." Artie gave her an odd look, like if she lived there, how come she didn't know the streets, but guessing that's the way of a girl.

"Sorry, mister, I'm just dog-tired. If you don't mind . . ."

Sitting in the chair by the window, turning her attention outside. After a while, Artie got up from behind the desk and went to a nearby lunch place, bringing her a cup of coffee. Thanking him, she drank it, then went back to pacing like she was caged.

When the woman passenger named Doris showed around six, Artie put her bags in the trunk, got them both into the car and started out of town. Sitting in back, Stella tried pushing off thoughts of Bennie, Artie speaking mostly to Doris, glancing across the seat now and then.

Keeping to herself, Stella looked out and watched the city fade, the bag between her feet. Wasn't long before she was feeling ill and asking Artie if he wouldn't mind stopping at the Conoco coming up on the right. Parking to the side of the pump, he waited for her to go to the ladies'. Coming back, she apologized, guessed it was on account of the coffee and hardly eating all day. Stopping at a place he knew, getting some sandwiches, Artie got underway again. Doris asked if Stella would rather ride up front.

"Don't make much difference, I just get woozy sometimes when I ride." Stella taking a bite of her chicken sandwich, saying, "Been that way since the time we rolled our Buick, right outside of Osage City."

"You were driving?" Artie said, guessing that explained the scar along her hairline.

"Was my husband driving, Johnny wanting to see if he could get the new Buick over a hundred. Could be a tire caught on something in the road, who knows, everything going like a blur." Stella smiled. She had guessed Bennie had spent a lot of their money on a new car and wrecked it on his way back to the motel that time, not knowing how to tell her. Likely stole the one he did show up in.

"So, you're married then?" Artie gave Doris a surprised look, glanced back at Stella.

She nearly said twice, instead saying neither of them had been hurt too bad in the crash.

"Glad to hear it," Doris said. "He in Topeka, your husband?"

"The two of us are going to New Orleans, maybe out to California. Gonna buy a house and settle and have kids."

"That sounds real nice," Doris said.

Stella turned her head to the window, trying to hide the crying.

Artie asked if she was okay. Doris digging in her bag for a hankie, passing it back.

"It's on account of what you were talking about," Stella said. "The FBI killing that poor man."

"Who, Bennie Dickson? Most wanted man alive ... well, he's gone now."

"Read how they indicted some politician on tax evasion, that man getting away with a lot more than Bennie Dickson ever saw from robbing a bank."

"One way to look at it, I guess." Artie turned to her, frowning again.

"Bet that politician's likely to end up in a country-club cell, you can bet on it."

"Never heard of any cell being like that," Artie said. "Not that I ever been in one. But I bet the law's fair enough."

"Ought to lock up the whole FBI, starting with that Hoover," Stella said, pressing her hands together.

"Well, no offense, but you ask me that man's a hero," Artie said. "Worst you can say maybe he's a bit eager."

"Ought to lock him up, and that woman in black too, the one who set him up."

"Who're we talking about?"

"Woman who lured Bennie. Bet she was working for the FBI, just like the one that lured Dillinger. Bitter women, getting them both killed."

"Don't know anything about that," Artie said. "Paper I read only talked about the woman who got away, Dickson's wife. Still looking for her."

"All that ink's just lies," Stella said, wiping at her eyes, didn't matter Artie was looking over the seat at her.

"Guess it's different times from when I was coming up." Artie gave Doris a glance, slowed the car and turned to Stella. "You don't mind me saying, you got some big ideas for a little girl, no offense, miss."

Looking at him, saying she was more grown-up than he'd believe.

"So, what's really in Topeka, miss, and how about the truth?"

"What are you saying?"

"Saying maybe you're mixed up in something. Maybe not thinking straight right now."

"Paid you my money, same as her. Told you I'm going to my folks', then seeing my husband."

Artie stopped himself reaching the paper next to him on the seat, the Dickson article talking about his wife, number two spot on the most wanted list. Said she slipped away when they got Dickson, said she was armed and dangerous. Then again, he'd had a couple nips earlier, and maybe he wasn't thinking straight. Best to keep his mind on the road.

"Just can't believe you're asking me all these questions," Stella said. "Well, I'm going to Topeka, and I'm arranging a funeral, if you got to know everything. Was my husband, killed in that car wreck I was talking about. Some things are just hard to talk about."

"Sure thing, miss. I'm real sorry." Artie glanced to Doris, Doris saying she was so sorry to hear it too.

The three of them sitting quiet, letting the miles clip past. Artie thinking about the photo he saw someplace of the Dickson couple, in better times at a carnival, trying to picture the girl in back with blonde hair.

Leaning her head against the window, Stella feigned sleep, not wanting to talk to them anymore. Remembering her birthday was coming, not wanting to spend it without him. Nearly a year since the two of them walked in that bank in Elkton. Sure didn't turn out like he promised it would.

Sitting there, refusing to believe he was gone, the hollowness of it inside her. Facing the window, she kept from crying, tried to keep herself from falling asleep, but after a while she drifted. Waking when she realized they had stopped along a row of houses. Doris was getting out in the dark, looking back and saying it was nice to meet her, and sorry for her loss, something more about time healing all wounds.

Stella thanked her for being kind.

Watching her disappear into the house, Artie asked, "So you got a spot in mind, miss, somewhere you want me to drop you for the night?"

"Want you to take me to Topeka, like you said." She sat up straight, felt her bag between her feet, saying, "That's the deal."

"Yeah, I know the deal, and I'll take you like I said, but we got a late start, and I could do with some rest. Not as young as you." After a moment. "Look, I'll drop you at a motel and pick you up first thing. We'll get some breakfast and start fresh."

"Can't be more'n an hour or so, I don't see not pushing through. Look, I just want to get home, mister."

"And home'll still be there by morning, and be one less car wreck for you to worry about. No offense, miss, I'm just tuckered. Plus I wouldn't want to drive into the teeth of some duster I can't see coming. More than one time I had to paste newspaper to the boards and windows to keep the sand and wind out my place. Them things are tough to make out at night, won't know it till they're right on you." Telling her the Congress Hotel was close and not so expensive.

"I look like I'm made of money? Wasn't counting on paying for no room." She looked at him and sighed. "Look, if it's all the same, I'll just stay in the car, sleep here."

It wasn't all the same, but Artie shrugged, still not sure about her, thinking her story didn't line up. And if she was the girl every lawman in the state was hunting, he could end up getting shot or arrested as an accomplice. Easing the car off the road, he pulled under the boughs of a couple of trees, a safe enough spot where they could spend the night. Didn't want to spend the night in the car with her, but didn't want to chance having his car stolen either. Saying, "You want the front or back?"

"Guess I'm fine where I am." Stella not happy about the delay, then saying, "If the cops come by, how about you just say I'm your wife? Be less questions that way."

More likely be his daughter, but Artie didn't want to talk to her anymore. The steering wheel tried to hog the front seat. Banging his knee into it throughout the night. Uneasy too, thinking of who she could be.

Stiff by early light, he got out and stretched, checking his wristwatch: half past seven. Had made up his mind about her. Looking in back as she sat up, blinking sleep from her eyes, telling him she was ready for Topeka.

"Got a little change of plans," he said.

"What change?" Stella pushed the door open, clutching her bag, but not getting out. "You said you'd take me to Topeka."

"First off, you said Kansas City, I'm sure you did, and here we are. Now, I'll go on to Topeka, but I'm gonna need another rider, make it worth the trip. Ethyl doesn't grow on trees, you know, not the last time I checked."

"At this rate . . ." Stella tossed herself back against the seat and pulled the door shut.

"Tell you what, there's an office close by. Just gonna stop and see if they got a rider. There's a bus stop at Tenth and McGee. If that suits you better, I can drop you. The bus comes first, then you just get on and ride. Be happy to give you the fare for your troubles. Call it my tough luck. And if it don't come by before I swing back with my other rider, then I'll take you right on to Topeka, and do it with a smile."

"Talking like I got a choice."

Driving to Tenth, Artie let her out at the bus stop, giving her the half-dollar fare. Glad to be shed of her, he forced a smile and wished her well. Funny, it never occurred to him last night, guessing on account he'd been drinking, that there ought to be a reward for information.

Didn't feel right to her, standing at the corner, not sure she could trust Artie Hoffman coming back for her. Crossing the street she went to the newspaper stand, stacks of newspapers, a rack of *Time*, *Life* and *Collier's* magazines, others lined below them. Asked the weathered man if he knew what time the bus came by. He said he only sold newspapers, didn't pay much attention to the bus, but reckoned it would be by, maybe within the hour or so, giving a shrug.

The *Kansas City Star* caught her eye. Couldn't help picking up a copy, looking at Bennie down on the sidewalk. Those four men standing in a line behind him, the caption calling them special agents, the looks on their faces like they bagged a trophy twelve-pointer, something Bennie used to talk about, taking her hunting deer. Tears fell onto the newsprint. Couldn't stop herself, Stella saying, "Sorry." Swiping at the wet marks.

"No need feeling bad for it, just another no-good," the old man said, leaning on his stand. "Going around murdering and robbing, the son of a . . . sorry about the language, miss, but them brave men did us a service, doing it in the line of duty. Was that Dickson crossed it and, well, that's what he got for it. Shame they didn't get his gun moll same time. Says she's just as dangerous and armed to the teeth, and a deadlier shot than he was. What kinda woman goes around like that, robbing and learning to shoot?"

"Never killed nobody, neither one of them."

"Well, don't know what papers you been reading, no offense, miss. But guess it's not something a nice girl ought to be troubling herself about anyhow. Just good to know the streets are safe for us to walk on. Uh, you buying?" The old man noting the tears on the paper.

She folded the paper, the photo of her beneath the fold. Looked different now from the old school photo, her with blonde curls back then. Seemed a lifetime ago. She set it down on the stack, paid him the three cents, said she was sorry about getting it all wet.

The old man nodded and wished her a fine day.

Re-crossing the street, she waited on the bus that never came. Seemed like forever, giving up on Artie Hoffman too, she walked back to the newspaper stand, asking about a travel agency nearby, the old-timer directing her to the A&A Agency over on Main. Walking to it, Stella stepped in, went to the desk and was told to have a seat. Surprised to see Artie pulling up out front of the door five minutes later with a woman in front of his Buick.

"You still want that ride?" Coming in, Artie smiled, apologizing for the delay, escorted her out and opened the back door, introduced the woman in front as Grace, said he had to pick up one more rider. Just a short hop back to Tenth, between Grand and Walnut. "You figure your directions and let me know where to drop you, okay?"

"Like I said, I'll know it when I see places." Stella thinking she'd get him to drop her on the fringe of town. Figure it out from there. She wanted to be with her mother, and she could stop up the block, keep watch on the house for a while, see if anybody was hanging around, keeping an eye out for her. Bennie had told her that lawmen were easy to spot, always looked like they were trying too hard to look natural.

She considered the seventy bucks she had in her bag was more than enough for food and a room for a couple of nights. Make a phone call to Liz and meet her someplace and get the package she had mailed to her, guessing it would take a few more days to get there. If that didn't work, she had the three rings and she could hawk the one, knowing she wouldn't part with the two wedding bands. Bennie gave her one as Mrs. Bennie Dickson, the other as Mrs. James Duncan. Smiling, thinking of him coming up with new names, even came up with the maiden name for her, Elva Clayton.

Spend some time at Mother's, then she could find her way out past Lake Benton, get the money Bennie buried at the railcar Spencer had dubbed Ben's cabin. Do it without anybody seeing her.

Then she'd catch a ride back to St. Louis, get that Mercury and drive out of there, back down to New Orleans, then maybe on to California. Have enough money to last long enough to get a new start going and figure things out.

Artie slowed at the curb, pulling her from her thoughts.

"This is the place." Looking up at a brick two-story, he said, "Be right back." And he was gone. Stella's eyes following him along the street.

"You from here?" Grace asked, turning on the seat, her eyes not meeting hers. "Me, I was born and raised right here in Kansas City. My, how it's changed since I was a girl."

"That so?" Stella could see Artie going up the block, looking back once and disappearing around the corner. Knowing she should jump out and hurry the other way. Just didn't have it in her to run anymore.

Grace went on talking about shops she liked, some new ones in place of ones that had been there one time. "How about you?"

"How about me what?"

"Oh, this city, you notice how much it's changed?"

"How much you getting?"

"What are you saying?" Grace turned to her, her eyes went wide, then she looked away.

"He promise you reward money, enough for a good day of shopping, that it?"

"Don't want a penny. Not sure why I'm here at all. Told him I didn't want to do it. Right now, I just want nothing to happen to you. You can believe that if you want."

Stella turned and looked out the window, some faraway voice saying it was the last chance, maybe it was his voice, telling her to get out of the car and beat it the other way. But she was done with all of it, she just wanted to go home. Getting an image of that roller rink and that time when he first skated up to her, said his name was Johnny. And all she did was fall in love.

Then there was Artie Hoffman coming back, four men coming behind him, fanning across the street. Saying to Grace, "Guess it takes four of them to catch a sixteen-year-old girl."

Grace didn't turn, just said, "Look, I'm sorry about the mess you're in, honey, but be a smart kid, alright? It can happen when you're young, you get mixed up with the wrong kind. Trust me, I know a thing about it. Papers call you wayward, from the wrong side of the tracks, but I can see you're alright, just mixed up is all. No offense. But listen to me, best thing you can do right now is whatever they say."

Stella snorted. "Got a backstabber giving me advice, being a friend to me now." She put her hand in the purse for the .38 that wasn't there. Needing him with her right then, to let her know what to do.

"Just show 'em your hands, honey. Let them take you."

Artie called for Grace to step out of the car, and she did it without another word, going over to him, her face against his chest.

The four men loomed like shadows around the car, boxing her in. Stella didn't look up when the hand tapped at her window, the man leaning in, saying his name, that he was a special agent.

"Yeah, what makes you that way, so special?"

Asking her to step out of the car, the man with his one hand behind his back, the way she remembered some waiter had done, some fancy place Bennie had taken her in New Orleans.

Then she was smiling up at this grown man with the nice tie and pomade in his hair, looking like he was afraid of her. Wondering what he'd do if she jerked her hand from the bag between her feet, nothing left to lose, and nothing left inside her. But she didn't do that, she just sat, even when he opened the door, reached in and took the bag from the floor, then taking her by the elbow and helping her out.

. . . thirty-five

Half an hour and she'd be counting the day's till and locking up. That shortness of breath coming again — the emphysema creeping up and getting worse these days. Looking away from the wall clock, Stella made sure the clerk was in the back, reaching the inhaler in her pocket, not wanting to let on. Her feet were throbbing like they always did by shift's end, Stella pushing that away too.

She'd drive home and let the dogs out in the yard. Always felt right being with them, patting and playing with them, watching them chase each other around the yard.

The day's date had been circled on the office calendar. Fifty years since he'd been gone — her Johnny — and she was thinking about him now, picturing him coming through the door of the Thriftway, the last customer of the day. Not as an old man of seventy-eight, but how he was back then. Outlining the handsome face and hearing those lines he laid on her the first time she set eyes on him. Still thinking of him as Johnny.

"Sixteen, huh? Well, I might've guessed older." Flashing her the honest blue eyes.

Stella seeing something behind that smile, this guy with the wavy hair, hanging around the roller rink, looking at her, then coming over to her by the boards. Making a fast stop and showing his moves. She smiled, thinking how she lied about her age, thinking she got away with it. Not much in her life she ever got away with, the reformatory years, then the marriage to Ralph the son of a bitch.

There never were any kids, something she and Johnny had talked about, the house with a yard, the dogs playing out back . . . well, she had that, the dogs and the yard.

Thinking of him took her back to the time in the women's joint at Alderson, meeting Kathryn, wife of Machine Gun Kelly, and Billie Jean Parker, Bonnie's sister, the three of them talking about the men, kidding around about forming a gang when they got out, show the boys how to do it right and get away with it.

Paroled in '49, first thing she caught a ride to the cemetery in Auburn, clearing weeds away from his stone, and saying a proper goodbye to her Johnny, expecting he knew she'd been held that cold April day when they buried him. Her parents and Liz attending. Liz coming to the jail after, telling Stella about all the flowers heaped up on his coffin, the two of them crying, unable to hold each other on account of the guards watching.

After her release, Stella went home to Mother and stepdad Lester, and lived in Topeka before Ralph the son of a bitch showed up in her life. And she lived with that mistake before the smarten-up and divorce. Then lived on her own, making up her mind there were no men around half as good as Johnny.

Shuffling from place to place and taking odd jobs before buying the house on Sycamore. Paying cash for it, and later on buying a couple more around Raytown, folks speculating how a store clerk managed to save enough for it, Stella getting wind of the tittle-tattle about stashed money the Dicksons had buried around the state, most of it never retrieved by the FBI. Something she never talked about again.

Neighbor ladies who stopped by for tea wondered why Stella drove as fast as she did, like she was being chased. Seeing her take her pistol down to the Missouri River and shooting at tins on posts. Stella winked and said, "Well, you never know ... but it sure beats sewing." The ladies looking at each other. None of them asking about the photo on the mantle, the one of Bennie and Stella at the Topeka Free Fair back in '38. Instead asking about all the dogs Stella kept about the place, Stella talking to them like they were folk, admitting they were better company than most people she ever met. The tea ladies giving each other an uncomfortable look.

Mostly, she kept to herself, but she never had anything against most folks — signing on as an activist and unionizing local grocery checkers, getting fair wages and working conditions at the Justrites and Thriftways. Betting that got old Hoover boiling, Stella mixed up in something as communist as organizing unions and doing it right under that man's nose.

Stepdad Lester had been gone when she hired the lawyer to file for the presidential pardon, another match she held to Hoover's butt. And in spite of the FBI's meddling, Nixon granted it full and unconditional. Something Alvie was still around to see, dying just three years back, buried in the family plot, a mile from where the Ace Motor Court had been.

Mother in the convalescent home, with not much time left. Something that would leave Stella on her own, but it wouldn't be too long, she didn't need the doctor to tell her that.

Looking at the clock again, she coughed into her fist and went to the door, switching the lock and flipping the sign in the window. Then she smiled, wondering even after all this time, whether he'd be waiting, sure he'd had enough time to come up with some new lines.

Acknowledgments

I n gratitude to my publisher, Jack David, who has always been encouraging. I've learned a great deal from him along the way. As well, to the amazing team at ECW Press. I always feel like everyone there is dedicated to making my book the best it can be.

It's a pleasure working with my editor, the meticulous and insightful Emily Schultz, who has been there from book one. Many thanks to Peter Norman for his razor-sharp copy editing, Lindsay Humphreys for her proofreading talents, and Michel Vrana for his creativity on the cover design.

As always, a big thank you to my wife, Andrea, who is the best sounding board, and ~~often~~ usually the voice of reason. And to my son, Xander, who is generous, supportive and a great friend.

In recognition to Bennie Dickson for his poem at the beginning of this novel, and to his great-niece, Amanda Dickson, for her kind permission to use it.

Lastly, I appreciate every reader, because without them …

ENVIRONMENTAL BENEFITS STATEMENT

ECW Press Ltd saved the following resources by printing the pages of this book on chlorine free paper made with 100% post-consumer waste.

TREES	WATER	ENERGY	SOLID WASTE	GREENHOUSE GASES
8	**660**	**3**	**28**	**3,550**
FULLY GROWN	GALLONS	MILLION BTUs	POUNDS	POUNDS

Environmental impact estimates were made using the Environmental Paper Network Paper Calculator 4.0. For more information visit www.papercalculator.org

This book is also available as a Global Certified Accessible™ (GCA) ebook. ECW Press's ebooks are screen reader friendly and are built to meet the needs of those who are unable to read standard print due to blindness, low vision, dyslexia, or a physical disability.

Get the eBook free!*
*proof of purchase required

Purchase the print edition and receive the eBook free!
Just send an email to ebook@ecwpress.com and include:

- the book title
- the name of the store where you purchased it
- your receipt number
- your preference of file type: PDF or ePub

A real person will respond to your email with your eBook attached. And thanks for supporting an independently owned Canadian publisher with your purchase!